STUCK TO YOU

Haven Nichols

Cover design by: Haven Nichols
Printed in the United States of America
Intended for mature readers (18+) due to intense scenes.

CHAPTER ONE

Robin

It's dark out, and the wind is blowing strong, sending chills down my spine. Our house is on fire because of a rich man, a man whose family is quite powerful, owning many companies around the world. The name of this family is called the Preuett's. For many years, they have been there for my family, helping us through some really tough times, which we don't ask for unless we're almost going bankrupt or close to. His dad, Conner, is my father's childhood friend, and Conner's son is mine. I'm now twenty-two, and he is twenty-five.

He fell in love with me, but I don't feel the same way. He didn't accept my rejection, so he burns my house and says he'll give us a new one to get what he wants. He wants to set up a company where my home is. My parents agreed, but I know the real reason. The man I'm talking about is Kris Preuett.

As we stand close to the road, watching the flames, a limo screeches to a stop behind us. My mother clapped her hands together excitedly and turned to the limo. I turn my head to them and watch them get in. "I'm not going, I think I'll live with my grandfather until I buy my own house!" Although I said that they didn't pay any attention, they just kept talking to one another. I stared at them and was about to walk off, but a sudden shove from behind pushed me into the limo. I flipped myself around to see who it was only to see a man, Rex, Kris's butler. "So sorry, but this is an order from master Kris.!" Then, the door shuts. Now, I'm stuck, stuck like a rat with nowhere to go.

After a while, the limo stops, Rex walks around and opens the door. We got out and a mansion is now in view. "You're here!" A man is walking toward us with open arms. My heart drops when I see the man... It's Kris. "Come, I'll show you to your new home!" We follow him to a house on the right side of the mansion. The house he brought us to looks big enough for at least twelve people to live in. "This is your new home, though to live here I do have one condition. Your daughter, Robin Lee, will live with me." Mother and father look at one another with big grins on their faces. Together they looked back at Kris and said, "We agree!"

"What! Don't I have a say in this?" I shouted in anger. No one answered, instead Kris said thank you and goodbye to my parents then walked away from the house pulling me along. I looked back, but my parents didn't say a word, they just watched with those silly little grins. I faced forward and was only a few steps away from the steps of the mansion. I struggled to loosen his grip on me only to find it tightened around my wrist. I ended up being dragged up the steps and into his home, but he didn't stop there. He pulls me up some more steps, then down the hall. All the tugging annoys me. "Can you let go? It hurts!"

He didn't say anything, didn't let go, nor look back. "Hello, did you hear me?" No answer. He pulled me into a room and pushed me into a wall. His hand pulled my arm above my head, his body pushed up against mine, holding me there. His brown hair falls over his blue eyes that are staring me down. "Now listen up, you will be living here with me! You will behave and do as I say! You can try to run, but you must know I'll always find you!" His voice was a little harsh as he said this. He lets go of my wrist and stands there for a bit before turning and leaving the room, shutting the door behind him. I slide my back down the wall dumbfounded, tilting my head back, and looking up. *'What on earth is going on?'* I close my eyes, feeling worn out.

'It's warm, why?' I sat up and looked around the room. *'When did I fall asleep?'* My hand bumped against something which made me freeze in place. I looked to where it was and saw Kris laying next to me. I jump back, almost falling off the bed. *'Crap! That startled me!'* Shaking a bit, I take a few deep breaths and try to calm down. Once I became calm, I looked back at Kris. Without realizing it, I began to be memorized by him. He has beautiful long eyelashes, and short wavy brown hair, and for some reason, I missed his blue watery eyes. "It's not nice to stare!" His eyes fluttered open. His eyes shimmered from the sunlight coming from the window and threw the silky white curtains. Amazed by his beauty, I didn't notice his arms sliding around my waist, next thing I knew he was pulling me into his embrace, making my heart beat fast. The tips of our noses are touching one another, I feel my face get hotter and hotter every second, as his breath brushes against my skin, and my mind goes blank. He leans in more, his lips lightly touching mine. *'Wait, no!'* I come back to my senses, placing my hands on his chest and trying to push him away, but no luck. *'He's too strong!'* I close my eyes tightly as his hand slides behind my head pulling in more, kissing me deeper. I teared up a bit, but right when I was about to give up, a knock came from the door. Our lips parted when he left, and he went to the door, twisting the doorknob and then cracking the door open.

"Master Kris, breakfast is ready!" Having said that, I

could hear Rex walking away and the door closed. I sat up then slid my legs off the bed. Standing up off the bed, head kept down as my cheeks burned from the thought of what just happened, I stumbled to the table near the window as Kris walked past me and started pulling out clothes. He grabbed out a nice short red dress and black heels before passing them over to me. He leans toward me, placing a kiss on my cheek before heading to the bathroom with the clothes he will wear. Once he's out of the room, I look over at the bed where the dress lay. I walk over and pick it up, inspecting it before putting it back down and stripping off my clothes. Once dressed, I go over to the bathroom and lightly knock on the door. "Um, Kris..." The door swings open, and Kris stands at the door wearing a black suit and a red necktie that matches my dress. *'He's so hot!'* He slides past me and heads over to the bed and picks up his shoes before sitting on the bed. Quickly, I slid into the bathroom and shut the door. *'Robin! What on earth are you thinking? You cannot fall for him, it's only a trick.... At least, I hope it is! I need to hurry and find a way to escape before I fall deeper!'*

As I'm just about finished with my hair a knock comes from the door. "Hurry up, we don't have all day!" He yells from the other side. My teeth are clean, my makeup is done, I finished up with my hair and swung open the door. I came out and saw him waiting for me, holding out his hand. "Come here!" I slowly place my hand in his and he pulls me over to the bed, setting me down. I look at him as he kneels and picks up one of my heels then slides it on my foot, he lightly touches my other foot and begins to slide on the other heel. “Tha... Thank you!” He stood there looking me over twice, grinning to himself. With my guard down, his arm wraps around my waist, tilting me back a bit, and kisses me. “You look amazing!” He then slides his hand in mine before we head down to the dining room.

I'm sitting at a dining room table that seems to be able to fit twenty people, but at the table, it's just me and Kris. I look around the dining room as waiters put food on the table. On the plate is an omelet, a side of grapes, and in the glass cup is water. I slowly dig in, keeping my head down. No words were spoken and it was kind of getting a tad a worrisom so I hurried to eat the food. "Well that was good, thank you! Know if you don't mind, I will be going kno-" "Master Kris, you have a visitor!" I get cut off as a maid enters the room. "Thank you, take them to my office. I'll be there in a minute." He stood up and handed the plate to Rex. "Yes sir!" She takes her leave and I try to follow, but Kris stops me in my tracks by grabbing my arm. "Where are you going?" His eyes darken which sends chills crawling up my spine. "T...To go see my mother and father!" I said in a shaky voice. He let go, but where he touched me I still felt the pain running through my arm. "Say hi for me!" He turns his back to me and then heads off to his office.

I walked to my parent’s new house and knocked on the front door. It slowly opened and a tall man stood at the door.

"Yes, what can I do for you?" "Um... I would like to see my mother and father please!" He steps back and lets me in. He shuts the door behind me. “Right this way milady!” He walks me to a room and then knocks on the door. "Master and Missus Lee, Miss Robin is here to see you!" "Let her in!" Once the door is open and arms wrap around me. "Robin, how are you? How's everything with Kris?" Their eyes twinkle with delight. "Terrible! Can't we just go buy another home or go live with my grandmother? Please, I don't want this! I only stayed here for one night and I'm already sick of this!" "Sweetie, I'm sorry, but we made a promise long ago and we can't go back on it now," Mother says, wrapping her hands around mine. "Listen, Robin, you may not like him now, but we believe you'll like him someday." My father pats my head. I reached up, pulled his hand off my head, and stepped back. "No, I won't! I will never fall for that man!" I take off my heels and throw them to the ground. I turned around and sprinted out the door and down the hall. “Robin!” My mother shouts! “Don't let her leave!” I can hear my Father’s screams at his butler. Once at the front door, I shoved a maid who was reaching for my arm. I grabbed the door handle and swung it open. “I’m sorry!” I shout as I run out of the house and to the gates, but I don’t stop there. I keep running and I don't look back even though my name is being called and they’re running after me, but they can't catch up to me.

After a long time of running, I finally lost them. Even though I’m already a safe distance away my legs won't stop and the same goes for my tears. My line of view is blurry from tears while my legs become worn out, my foot catches against my leg, tripping me. I fall, slamming my face into the hard ground below. I tried to stand up, but my legs gave up on me, making me go back to the ground. I push myself up onto my knees, feeling something wet and cold slide down my face, I place my hand on my head flinching a bit. "Are you ok?" A man walks up to me and holds out a hand. The man has dark black hair and dark green eyes. I could see his abs through his tight black shirt, his biceps tearing through his sleeves. *'Is he an angel?'* I slowly reached for his hand, but before I could touch it everything went black. I could feel my arm give up and my body begin to fall but was then stopped in mid-air and it felt as if I was floating.

Finally, coming too, I sit up, as my head begins to throb. "Are you feeling ok?" A man walks up to me and sits on the edge of the bed. He sets a bowl of soup on the nightstand. "Yes, thank you very much!" "Names Jack, and you are?" He put his hand out to me and I shook it. "Robin!" "Well Robin, you can stay here until you're ready to get back on your feet. My mother put clothes at the end of the bed for you." He smiled at me and left without saying a word. As the door shuts, I sit for a bit to collect my thoughts, then slowly get out of bed and take off my clothes. I pick up the clothes that are laid out for me. I put on a pink flowery shirt and a black flowy skirt then went up to the mirror to fix my light blonde hair, but as I was putting it up, a bandage on my head caught my green eyes. Sliding a finger over it, sending a sharp pain. Tears trickled down my cheeks.

I shook my head and put a big smile on my face. "No, there's no need for tears!" I tell myself, I walk over to where the bowl of soup is and pick it up, the smell of chicken smells good. I quickly ate the soup till there was nothing left, after I looked back at the door. With the dishes in hand, I walked over to it. With my free hand, I grip the knob and slowly twist it open then step out of the room. I walked down the hall straight into the kitchen.

I see a woman standing by the stove. She turns and puts the pot in the sink. As she did this, it seems she has spotted me from the corner of her eyes. "Finally awake dear?" She says to me in a sweet voice. "Yes, thank you for the clothes and everything else." I go over to place the bowl in the sink before heading to sit down at the dinner table. "You're very welcome!" A thought crossed my mind and I asked the woman, "How long have I been unconscious?" She turns to the table and sits across from me. I examined her figure, she has long wavy black hair, and her eyes were the same green as her sons. *'So pretty, I can see where Jack got his looks!'* "Oh, about three days!" I snapped out of my daze after hearing what she said. "He still hasn't found me?" I said under my breath. "What was that dear?" the woman asks. "Ah oh no, it was nothing! Um uh, I...I'm Robin and you are?" I say holding out my arm out over the table. "Elizabeth Phinks or Mrs. Phinks will do." She reaches out and shakes my hand. Jack walked in with a box with the words “noodles” on it and set it down on the dinner table. I look at Mrs. Phinks and ask, "Do you own a restaurant?" She looks at me with a big smile on her face. "Yes we do, and it's a noodle restaurant." I sat up a little straighter. "May I please work there to pay back all your kindness? I will work hard!" She jumped out of her set, grabbed my hands, and tightly held them together between hers. I looked at her and it looked as if flowers were blooming behind her. "Yes!" She shouts with joy. "I would love some help around here because the only people working are me and my son Jack. You see, this restaurant belongs to my husband Patrick Phinks. It was his pride and joy, so ever since he died we just couldn't part with it." She lets go and goes through a door twirling and humming a little tune. "I haven't seen her this happy for a long time!" Jack says, coming over to me, stretching out his hand. "Come!" I grabbed his hand and he led me through the door Mrs. Phinks went through.

Outside the door is their restaurant, where Mrs. Phinks and Jack work. I could smell a wonderful smell coming from a pot Mrs. Phinks was in front of, but then the bell rang. It comes from another door. I followed Jack to where it came from, in that room was the dining area. The walls are lime green, the tables are light brown, and a light brown bar. Jack walks up to a table where a man is sitting, he begins to talk to the man and is writing something down on a piece of paper. He comes to me and hands me the paper as another customer walks in. "Can you hand this to my mother for me?" I took it from him and he walked off. I go to the back and hand it over to her and another ring echoes in the room. "Would you like to help Jack out?" She asks. "Yes, I would love to!" She hands me a notepad and pen and I go straight to work with a bright smile on my face.

Days have passed and Kris still hasn't found me. I slowly started to forget about him and my problems back home. I have been working at Jack's family noodle restaurant for three weeks now and it's a fun job. "Robin, can you take this to table four?" Mrs. Phinks calls from behind the bar. I grab it and start walking to the table and set it down for the guests then walk back for the next plate of food, smiling happily. *'It's so nice here!'*

The day slowly goes by. Jack runs up to me as I leave the table. "Robin, You can go ahead and quit for the day, I'll do the rest and lock up." He says this with a warm smile. "Ok!" I turned and walked back to the door of the restaurant kitchen then through the door that leads to the house and walked to my room. I grabbed the nightgown Mrs. Phinks bought me and went to take a bath. I turn on the water, take off my clothes and wait for a while until steam rises from the tube, then slip in. Laying there, I soak in the water, letting the water consume me, my eyes closed. After a bit, I stand and drain the water, turn on the showerhead, and wash my hair, face, and body. When done, I get out of the tube and put on my nightgown, then dry my hair, and brush my teeth. I stared at my head through the mirror, then slowly touched a finger to where the cut once was, but even though the wound was gone, I still felt a sharp pain. I turn and go out of the bathroom, fall on the bed, and close my eyes with an arm laying across my face. A knock comes from the door which makes me jump. Mrs. Phinks poked her head through the crack. "Are you going to sleep, dear? You did a great job today, Jack's already in his bed asleep. He looked very tired today. Well, have a good night's rest tonight, because you'll have to wake up extra early tomorrow before Jack does because you see, tomorrow is going to be his twenty-third birthday, so we have to get everything ready." A smile crosses my face. "Ok, I'll do my best to help!" After that, Mrs. Phinks seemed to shine brighter than ever when I said that. "Well I should probably leave you alone now, you must be tired. Good night dear!" "Good night!" I say back as she leaves the room. I slip under my covers as a slight giggle slips through my lips. I lay there for a bit staring at the ceiling then closed my eyes and dreamed away.

"Rise and shine, today's the day!" Mrs. Phinks comes running in, pushing open the curtains to the window. I rise off the bed as she shoves a light pink dress and white heels on me, then hurries me to the bathroom. "Hurry up and get ready, then come help!" She shuts the door in a rush. I stare for a sec then turn on the water. I waited for the hot water to kick in, pulled the shower valve, slipped in, closed the curtain behind me, and took a quick shower. Once done, I get out and dry off before putting on the clothes, then blow dry my hair, and right when I am about to fix it, Mrs. Phinks comes in and asks, "Can I do your makeup and hair, dear?" "Yes, I would love that!" I responded. She leaped in glee and pulled me over to my vanity, sat me down, turned me where I couldn't see what she was doing, and started to do my hair. After that, she did my makeup and turned me to the mirror. I was speechless. My light blonde hair was very wavy and had a little puff on top. My green eyes popped out from the light pink eyeshadow and my eyelashes were very long. "Do you like it?" She asks with both hands on my shoulders and her head right next to mine. "Like it? I love it!" I get up with excitement and with a big smile on our faces, we go out the door and down the hall into the restaurant, where there were a lot of friends and family, and go straight to work.

After a couple of minutes, we finished setting up for the party, and right when we finished a man, one of Mrs. Phinks's friends, came running in from the house door into the kitchen screaming "He's coming!" We turned off the lights and waited. A swing of the door and the lights flicker back on, and letting go of our breaths we shout, "Surprise!" Jack hesitated for a second then smiled. "Thank you all!" Me and Mrs. Phinks begin to sing "Happy Birthday", our voices rise as others chime in. Mrs. Phinks set the cake on the bar next to him and at the end of the song he blows out the candles. "Happy nineteenth birthday sweetie!" Mrs. Phinks says.

Near the end of the day, people leave one by one, and I go ahead and start picking up the trash and the dishes. As I work going from one table to the next, I jump when strong arms wrap around my waist and a face buried into my neck. "What's wrong Jack?" I ask. "Just let me hold you for a bit please." We stand there, with no movement, no sound. I can feel butterflies flutter in my stomach.

That night as I laid in bed, slumber would never hit. Thoughts of the day played in my mind causing my emotions to be all over the place, my face burning with heat along with the places Jack had held me.

CHAPTER TWO

Kris

'So she thought she could escape me?' It only took a few days to investigate where she had disappeared too and if it wasn't thanks to the cameras down the road I wouldn't have caught her savior and her misfortune. *'This clumsy girl had tripped trying to run from me and had knocked herself out!'* Pacing the floor I contemplated what I should do, though it really didn't take long for me to come up with an answer, one that caused me to let out a heavy sigh. *'If it's freedom she wants, it's freedom I'm giving until she either comes back to me or until I've had enough. I know this girl and she can be quite stubborn!'*

A couple of weeks in and she hasn't returned. As I'm reading through the company's reports I can't help but smile thinking of her working in a restaurant and how she might have been stumbling over her own two feet the whole time.

Part of me really wants to go see her work in action, especially how she would react to serving me. No, it's not like she's never worked before, but most of her jobs were in retail and due to her slip ups they mostly kept her at the registers... So maybe I had intervened a few times having them keep her in that position, but that was only because I was looking out for her.

My eyes trail to the photos on my desk, a picture of Robin serving food to a couple sitting at a table. I sit there for a good few minutes in a daze until a sudden burst through the door brings back my attention. One of my men walks into the room. Finn, one of the bodyguards I have follow Robin. "Sir, I'm here to give our daily reports!" He gives a light bow towards me. "Ah Finn, let's see it!" I stretch out my hand to him as he passes over his and Aaron's detailed notes on Robin and those she is around, along with more photos. *'These photos...'* My grip tightens on the documents and anger rises inside me. I storm around my desk slamming papers into Finn's chest while crushing the picture in my other hand before dropping it to the floor, allowing it to slowly un-crumble, revealing an intimate moment between a man and my woman.

I'm almost out the front door when Rex sprints up next to me, following. "Is everything ok sir?" "Get in the car, we are picking up my fiancé! I think it's time she's learned what happens to bad girls when they act up!"

CHAPTER THREE

Robin

The door to the restaurant opened, the bell echoing through the store. "Sir, we are closed!" Mrs. Phinks says to the stranger. "Oh, I'm sorry, but I'm not here to eat. I'm looking for a woman!" *'That voice... I know that voice.'* Trembling, I grip Jack's shirt as my breathing becomes unstable. “She goes by the name Robin! Robin Lee!” The arms around me tightened, crushing my stomach. Jack releases me after a while and seems to come to a resolution after sensing my fear. "Go and hide!" He says. I nod my head and scurry around a corner, peeking from the side.

Jack turns back around and walks over to Kris. "I'm sorry, but there is no one here by that name." He says. "Then you wouldn't mind if I look around." A sly smile crawls across Kris's face. "And what rights do you have!" Jack crosses his arms. "It seems you don't know who I am. My name is Kris Preuett, son of Alex and Clare Preuett." Kris's introduction froze them solid. "Uhh... Well, do you have any proof?" Jack said finally.

As I watched, I could see this would not end well. "Come in!" Mrs. Phinks says, pushing her son away. "Thank you!" Kris comes in. Jack tries to charge at him but is still held back. I look down, beginning to hyperventilate again. *'Should I go back?'* "There you are!" My arm gets pulled and I fall onto someone's chest.... Kris's chest. I look up at his blue eyes with fear, shaking. "Don't touch her! Can't you see she doesn't like you?" Jack struggles against his mother, his eyes locked on Kris.

Kris doesn't say anything. "Well!" Jack adds. Kris smirks ear to ear. "Hmmm!" With my hand attached to his, he turns and walks a few steps toward Jack and his mother. "It seems you don't understand. This woman is my fiancé, so that makes her my property. She doesn't have a choice in this matter. Oh! And if you want her, you'll have to kill me first." I quiver, tears fall from my eyes, and I bite my bottom lip. *'Property, are you freaking kidding me!'* While out of it he pulls me in, his lips pressed up against mine. My eyes went wide, and my hands flew to his chest struggling to push him off, but there was no luck. His arms wrapped around my waist, pulling me in more. “Please leave! I don't want to hear anymore." Mrs. Phinks says, looking down. Our lips parted, leaving a big smile on his face. I heard Mrs. Phinks take a deep breath and then look at me. "I don't want to see you ever again." I began to quiver, my legs becoming weak, but I was quickly relieved when she gave me a quick wink so I know she doesn't mean it, one Kris didn't see.

"Goodbye, and thank you!" Kris pulled me towards the door, but I was free from the grip when Jack pulled my arm back, forcing me to fall into his embrace. "I don't want you to go. I love you, Robin." He squeezes me tightly, his face buried into my neck once more. I feel the butterflies grow and my legs get weak by the second. "I love-" "Ok that's enough." I was cut off, pulled away, and thrown over his shoulder. "Stay away from my women!" That's all Kris says and walks out the door. "Robin, I'll come for you! Wait for me!" Jack yells. "I love you!"

He sat me down when we got to his limo, but was quickly shoved in and followed by Kris. I scoot away from the man. He doesn't say anything, he just stares me down, it feels like blades are being thrown at me. I crouched myself into a ball not caring about his presence.

"Welcome back master Kris and miss Robin." I hear Rex's voice echo in the car as he opens the door. "Robin, come here!" Kris touches my arm with the tip of his fingers. I don't move. No words escaped my lips. "ROBIN!" His booming voice makes me jerk in my spot. I slowly move and slip out. My bottom lip quivers as tears still fall down my face. *'Why? Why did I have to be childhood friends with him? Why me?'*

As we walked up to his home, I was stopped in my tracks when two bawling parents wrapped themselves around me. "Oh my... My baby! Where... Where have you been?" My mother breathes out between her sobs. "Please never run away again!" My father says. *'Them crying like this, it's my fault! I never meant to hurt them, but I don't want this! Who wants to live a life where they're forced to be with this man?'* "Mother! Father! I'm sorry," I say, faking a smile. "but I don't want to be with Kris." They back up, taking their warmth with them. "I'm sorry, but you don't have a choice." My father breathes looking down, as well as my mother. *'Ahhh! It's this again!'* "But why? This is my life, is it not?"

"It is, it's just...." Mom trails off making my nerves start to grow. "It's just what?" I ask. Mother and father look at each other, then dad looks back at me and opens his mouth. "When you were in your mother's womb, my company went bankrupt. We slowly lost everything. One by one things were lost and soon there was going to be nothing left and we were leading you into a dark life. Thank heavens angels descended upon us, Mr. and Mrs. Preuett, offering us a deal that they would help us. The deal was for us to give you to their son when they thought the age was right." My mind went blank.

Back in my... Well, I guess you can say my prison being that the door is locked because they don't trust me, which I see why, but it's been a few days and it's beginning to feel stuffy in my room and it's boring. Even so, I refuse to talk to Kris and the servants. I sit there on my bed with a dead look and haven't touched my food. "You're not eating?" Kris comes into the room sitting next to me. "Robin! Speak to me! Please!" He reaches an arm out to me. "Don't touch me!" I scream. When I did I seemed to have made him snap because I could feel the side he was sitting on boiling. He quickly stands up again. "It's your fault that you're here. If you hadn't run away none of this would have happened." He yells.

I turned my head not wanting to see him, but he gripped my chin and turned my face back to him. "Don't look away!" He gets to eye level with me trying to calm himself down. "Listen, I was worried about you!" His eyes softened with sadness. "Please don't run away again!" That said, he leaned in, but before he could do anything, I closed my eyes tightly and bit my bottom lip, tensing up. I waited for his lips to crash into mine, but it never came. I slightly raise my eyelid to see a very depressed look and him backing away, then leaving the room. Releasing the tension, and letting go of my breath, I lay on the bed.

Running... Running down a pitch-black hallway, not going anywhere. "Robin!" My name echoes in the room. "Robin!" Fear grows and beads of sweat cover my body. "Go away!" I scream, tears streaming down my face as I run from the unknown. Then, right when all hope was lost, a light appeared and there I saw him. "I'm here Robin," Jack says, holding out his arms. "Come here." I dive his way. "Jack!" "Oh no, you don't!" I was pulled back, and the darkness engulfed the light and along with Jack left me with the beast. "I won't let you leave!" Arms swarmed around my body like vines and lips forced on mine. I tried to shove him off, but I only got a glimpse of his face till his lips covered my mouth once more... It's Kris. Our lips part once again, but only an inch. "You are mine!"

"Nooo!" I sat up, breathing hard. I look around the empty room. I quickly got off the bed and ran to the bathroom, splashing cold water all over my face. I'm not scared, but sad, depressed.... Ok, maybe I'm a bit scared! I don't want to be engaged to a man who gets what he wants by force and calls it his property. Kris has forced me here, called me property like I'm a thing that you can buy with money, took away my freedom and he took me away from something I cherished. Calming down a bit, I turn to the tub and turn on the faucet, letting the tub fill up with warm water, then strip off my clothes. I turn the faucet off and slip in, letting the water cover me and wash away the sweat. *'So relaxing!'* I sink a bit further where my whole head is almost under. "Robin!" A knock comes from the door as well as a man's voice. I jump and hurry for a towel, then push against the door locking it. "Yes! What do you want?" I asked, hanging my head. "I thought I heard you scream, so I came to check on you." "I'm fine!" I say, answering. Nothing! He doesn't say a word. As I lean on the door I hear the shuffling of his feet and a door shutting. Once I believe he's gone I got back in the bath and scrubbed my body from head to toe. When done, I slip out, plug in the blow dryer, dry my hair, then brush my teeth. After that, I go back to my room and up to a drawer, pull out a pair of shorts, underwear, and a t-shirt and slip it on, then straight back to bed.

I lay on my side, close to the edge of the bed, the side near the door to the room, the light from the window covered by a black cover I put up, also covering the white silky curtains. All is silent, I start to drift off once more. Suddenly, something warm locked around my body and pulled me into an embrace making me fully awake of my surroundings. I can't move! Lips touch my neck, sending chills up my spine. "Stop..." I struggle, but his grip gets tighter. I close my eyes feeling his lips claim my neck and hear a light moan, "Robin!" Tears slipped through my eyes as he turned me on my back and covered me with his body. His lips forced onto mine, kissing me deeply. "Mmmmm!" I pushed against him, but no luck. His hands crawl on my body over my clothes. Fear grows and without a second thought...

He flinches and sits up, still over me. I look at him. Something cold is on my lip and red drizzles down his chin from his bottom lip. He slips away to the edge of my bed and looks down at the ground, letting the cut still drip, staining the sheets and the carpet, along with his clothes. I sit up and backed away. "Why do you hate me? Why won't you love me? What's so good about that guy Jack and what does he have that I don't?" He clenches his teeth in anger and stands. "I can get you whatever you want! Makeup, jewelry, clothes, you name it and it's yours!" His voice rises, eyes darken. "Tell me! What can that commoner give you!" That word "commoner" made me burn. I step off the bed and walk right up to him and punch his chest. "I'm a commoner too you jerk. I'm not rich and I'm fine with it." I punched him repeatedly... but he didn't stop me.

“Sorry!" I stopped mid-punch. "I shouldn't have vented my anger like that." His eyes turn soft and he slightly smiles. He looks like he's going to cry. I let out a deep sigh, walked closer, and hugged him. "It's ok," *'Man I'm a softy when I see that!'* That was always the card he had used since we were little. "But can you please give up on me? I'm never going to feel the same way you do. You have always been family, like a big brother. Nothing more, nothing less!" "I don't care!" He wraps his arms around me and squeezes. We stayed this way for a while.

Growling echoes throughout the room, and my face flushes in embarrassment. "Oh right, the main reason I came was to bring you to dinner." We separate and he drags me through the door and down the stairs, then to the dining room. *'Wait... Am I aloud out?'* He sets me at the table and takes a seat across from me. "I thought we could eat together. I'm finished with all my work and thought it was getting a bit stuffy in that room." A feast was laid out on the table, lids still on. He lifts the lids and puts food on mine and his plate, then sits back down and digs in. I picked up my fork and also dug into the food, speedy shrimp pasta, pork chops with raspberry sauce, simple fried morel mushrooms, honey-roasted red potatoes, and grilled beets in rosemary vinegar. "I also thought once we finished dinner we could take a stroll in the garden." I stop and look at him with glittering eyes. *'I can go outside?'* Hiding my excitement I nod. "Ok!"

We finish dinner and head out the doors that lead out into the cold night. I grabbed the knob and almost went out till Kris grabbed me. "It's cold out tonight. Do you not want to put something a bit warmer on." He gestures towards my shorts and my t-shirt. "I'm ok." And before another word, I'm out the door and onto the patio in front of the rose garden. The thorn bushes are covered with red roses. The moon shines on the trail in between the roses, luring me in. I leap off the patio and run down the path, feeling the wind blow through my hair. I run and run through the rosy maze till I hit the hidden secret that lies in the center of it all. A small field full of flowers, a swing hung from a fully bloomed tree and a pond that shimmered from the moonlight. *'It's very peaceful. I feel like I've been here before.'*

"Beautiful, isn't it?" Kris says, coming from behind. "Do you remember when we were little? We used to come out here all the time. We picked flowers and made a wreath for each other, I pushed you on the swing, and sometimes we would go swimming in the pond. And at night when all the fun died down, not wanting to go home, we lay on the grass and watched the stars. As we lay, you would fall asleep. I would carry you home!" I listened, and slowly the memories came back to mind. He walks forward and turns halfway, holding out his hand. "Come! I'll push you!" I grabbed it and walked hand in hand to the swing. I sit on it as he gets behind me, placing his hands on my back. With one push I went forward in the swing. Again and again, this repeats itself, but I only go as high as his chest with every push. After a bit, I began to feel a thumping inside my chest. *'What's this feeling in my chest? It hurts!'* I grip my chest as I fly through the night. Slowly my heartbeat speeds up and my face becomes red. "Can I get off?" I ask. I feel the swing slow down till it stops. I quickly scurried off. My heart rate slowed down a bit and my face cooled. "You ok?" Kris asks, putting his hands on my shoulders, and right there my heart speeds up and my face burns again. *'What's going on?'*

"Y...Yes, I'm fine!" I move away, making his hands fall back to his side and the pain, as well as the heat, dies again. I walk toward the pond and sit on the ground. I sat there alone for a few minutes, hearing nothing but nature. I look out to the pond, slowly getting a bit drowsy. "Robin!" I jumped when Kris said my name. "Yes!" "May I give you something?" I tilted my head a bit to the side. "Sure!" "Close your eyes!" I do what I'm told without a thought. *'I'm getting sleepy!'* "There!" I open my eyes... Nothing. I looked around, and then I felt it. There was something in my hair. I slowly took it off to see a flower wreath. A slight giggle escaped my lips as I put it back on. *'He's still like a child.'* I look at him as he smiles down at me. "Thanks!" His smile grows a bit wider on his face. He sits next to me then we both lay side by side staring at the stars like when we were little. It was wonderful! As we lay there, slowly I drifted away into a peaceful slumber.

"Mmmm!" I sit up and rub my eyes. "I slept so well last night!" I say in a yawn, stretching my body feeling my bones crack, then relaxing once more. "Nock, nock! Can I come in?" I hear Kris say, his hand hitting the door. I stare at him as he slips in and brings a tray of food in his hands. "I'm not eating in the dining room?" I sit up as he lays the food on the room table. "I thought we could eat together here." *'I don't know why, but for some reason I'm enjoying this and he has been nice to me. Even so, I'm still upset with the way he took me away from Jake and locked me up for a while!'* I look at him. For some reason, I feel like we're children once more. *'He's still messy like when we were kids.'* I giggle as I grab a napkin and reach an arm to his face, whipping off the crumbs on the side of his lips.

I freeze in my position. *'What am I doing?'* I pull away and sit back in my seat eating once more. I look up between bites seeing him stare at me, his face a bit flushed. A thumbing begins once more in my chest. *'This again!'* With my free hand, I gripped my chest. It won't stop! Faster and faster my heart began to bang and my face burned. *'What does this mean? No, it can't be that I like him.'* I ate faster, down to the last bite, then I gulped down my drink, and walked off. The pain in my chest calmed and the heat on my face cooled as I walked away from Kris. *'Oh my gosh! I have feelings for Kris.'*

CHAPTER FOUR

Robin

"You ok?" Kris says from behind, touching my shoulder, making the reaction happen again. I tighten my eyes and squeeze my chest "Don't touch me!" I screamed, swatting his hand away. I can feel him jump from my sudden outburst. My bottom lip quivers and tears stream down my face. " I hate you!" And I ran out. Down the stairs, out the front door into the yard. I ran next door to my family's home bursting through the door and ignoring the butler and maids. Entering their living room I fall onto a couch balling into the cushions. "Sweetie!" My mother comes rushing in behind me. She sits on the edge of the bed and rubs my back. "What's wrong dear? Did you get into a fight? Are you hurt?" I sat up, eyes puffy and red. "Mother, I'm a terrible person and I'm confused about how I feel." I grabbed her and buried my face in her shoulder, crying like a kid. "Why do you say that?" She brushes my hair out of my face. I look into her brown eyes. "I don't understand my feelings! I love Jack, but why does my heart race for another?"

I see her sitting up straight. "You're in love with Kris!" She stands and then paces the floor in excitement. "Oh dear, we need to get things ready, like your wedding dress, your cake! Oh! I must go tell Jade!" "No!" I jumped in front of her waving my hands in her face. "You must not tell Mrs.Preuett! I still don't understand what I feel!" She grabs my hands and clamps them together. "That doesn't matter! What matters is that you do have feelings for Kris!" And with that said, she leaves the room in a hurry.

My hands drop to my side. *'Mom's no help!'* I sat with a huff and laid back down. After I lay there for a few minutes I stood and headed for my father's office, hoping he would listen to me, but I stopped around the corner as voices echoed in the room. "Hun, I just called Kris to let him know Robin is here!" “Good, now Jade, we need to talk about our children!” My mother says on the phone, sitting down on the couch in my father's office. "This is so exciting! When should the wedding be?" I hear Mrs. Preuett’s voice ask as my mother puts the call on speaker for my father to hear. "Ummm! How about next week in the rose garden where the kids used to play? Oh, that would be so cute!" My mother suggests. *'They don't care how I feel!'* I look down and walk back toward the living room then straight to the kitchen where the back door is. Out the door, it leads into the garden, with a gate that leads to the woods, where my dad and Mr. Preuett like’s to go hunting. I walk through the trees not caring where the path leads.

I'm far and lost! I sit by a stream and gaze at my reflection as tears stream down my face. "Please stop running from me!" I jumped with a sudden surprise but quickly shied away again. I plunged my face into the river not wanting him to see my puffy eyes, but was soon pulled back and held into a sudden embrace. "What are you doing?" He yells, holding me tight. "Are you trying to kill yourself?" My lip quivers. I try to hold back my tears. "Kris, please stop!" I pushed him off and showed him a fake smile. "I'm fine! I'm just a bit confused!" "About what?" He stares at me with his sad eyes. I say nothing and turn my back to him, walking in whatever direction is home. "Let's go back!" He wraps his arms around my legs and back, picking me up. “Rest a bit, I’ll take you back!” With him saying that, as much as I fought my eyes from drooping, I rested my head on his chest and fell asleep.

At home, I groggily sat up in my bed rubbing my eyes. I looked around the room to surprisingly not see Kris anywhere. Swinging my legs off the edge of my bed and placing my feet firmly on the ground. I stood and wobbled to the door, still exhausted. I called for a maid and asked her to let my parents know I'm home to find out Kris is one step ahead of me. She began to tell me all that Kris had told her to tell me when I awoke. After he laid me in my bed and headed off to my parent's home to report to them that I'm safe and while there he found out about our mother's plan for the wedding and how I have feelings for him. After he heard the news he left in a hurry to get a suit and wedding dress for me. He even ordered a wedding planner for us!

The worst part of it all is there are only six days till the wedding! I sit there in my room looking through my glass window watching the sun go down. *'Man the day went by fast!'* The pain in my chest grows as more tears trickle down my cheek. Filling the water, I quickly wipe it away and shake my head. "No! No more tears!" I rise and walk to the bathroom sink and splash my face multiple times with cold water, then look face-to-face with my reflection. The water drips off my face taking the place of my tears. I reach for a towel and wipe the water off.

"Robin! I'm back!" Kris's voice echoes in the room and soon his head pops from the doorway to the bathroom. "Are you feeling ok?" He looks at me with concern. I bring myself to smile. "I'm fine!" With that, he too smiles. He puts out his hand. "Come here!" He pulled me to my bed, sat me down, and told me to close my eyes. I sit there listening to a bit of the movement that echoes in the room and soon comes to a stop. "You can open your eyes!" I looked up at him and saw in his hands a white wedding dress and high heels. "That's not all!" He sets it down and reaches into his jacket pocket, pulling out a small box. *'No!'* He gets down on one knee. *'Please don't!'* He opens the box and what lies inside is a ring. *'Oh my gosh!'* "Robin! Will you marry me?"

Tears again come down. I'm speechless. "Please say yes!" "I...I... I can't!" His smile slightly fades. "What? Of course, you can! Our feelings are mutual." He opens his arms with a confused sad look. "No! Not fully! I still have feelings for Jack." His arm slowly lowers. "I'm sorry, but I really can't marry you!" I said that, but he wouldn't accept it. Kris's blue eyes darken. He came close, grabbing my arm, squeezing. "You will marry me! No matter what!" His gauze does not quiver. It's very stern. His grip on my wrist gets tighter and tighter. "Ahh!" He jumps when I yelp in pain, making him let go. Leaving a red mark on my wrist, which I know cradle with my other hand. He stares at the mark with regret, then looks away. "Goodnight!" With that, he leaves.

I lay on the bed in silence, not one tear falls, but my eyes are puffy. I know I can't run, but I can't go through with the wedding either. The days fly by now, giving me only two days left till the wedding, so I must hurry and figure something out quickly. I sit up, taking a deep breath and letting it out. All I know for now is that I can't keep moping here. I go up to the door and throw it open. Then with one step, I was stopped. A tall man with blond hair and another man, a bit shorter than me with red hair, both wearing a black suit, glasses, and a headset. "Hello, miss! We are your new guards. I'm Finn and this is Aaron! We were ordered to go wherever you go!" The tall guard, Finn, tells me. "I'm OK! I'm not going to try to run away, so there's no need." I walk around them and head down the hall. With every step I take, I hear another pair of footsteps behind me. I ignored it and went straight to Kris's office.

"Can you please take these guards away!" I said, walking into the office, but found it empty. *'Now what!'* I roll my eyes with a sigh and look at the two figures that are following me. "Where's Kris?" I ask. "In the garden," Aaron answers back. I stare at the two men. *'I wonder!'* I slowly slip past them again and walk with a skip in my step giving me some distance and when I am far enough, I slip around a corner, running down the hall. "Hey! Stop!" The two men yell out to me, but I don't stop. I zoomed down the stairs and out the back door. I look back to see the men slowing down, faces red and I can hear them breathing hard.

A smile creeps on my face with a small chuckle. “Oomph!” I see the sky go further from me as my body starts to fall, but I am caught mid-way. "You might want to be careful of where you're going." Kris is in front of me, arms wrapped around my waist, holding me up. "Sir... We're sorry...." The guards said finally catching up. Aaron falls to the ground and Finn hovers over his legs, breathing very heavily. "Try not to let this happen again!" Kris says then drags me to a table. He sits and pulls me into his lap. "Know! Where were we?" I see him looking across the table. I follow his gaze to see a man, with a gray beard, brown-grayish hair, and brown eyes, wearing a black hat and black suit with a white tie, and a woman, with blond-grayish hair and green eyes wearing a long yellow dress and white sun hat, sitting on the other side. The three people start to talk about politics and governmental things.

I sit there on Kris's lap in confusion, I don't quite understand what they're talking about. I gaze around trying to avoid all contact so they don't ask me anything about my opinion on this stuff. As I look, I spot a figure through the bushes. I tried to stand to go see what it was, but the arm around my waist would not loosen. "Kris darling! Do you mind me taking a few roses? It's so beautiful and would be perfect for my bath!" A voice yells from the bushes, then out pops a woman. She runs up with many roses in her hands. The girl gets closer and closer, and as she does her smile slowly fades.

"Who is this?" She points to me, her collection of roses falling to the ground. "Finally!" Kris pushes me off and stands, grabbing my hand in his. "I would like to introduce to you, my fiance Robin Lee. Robin, this is Lexi and Gary Smith, and their daughter Courtney." I look Courtney over. She has long blond hair and brown-black eyes, wearing a long light blue dress and black heels. "Ah! Umm! Hello!" I say feeling a little flustered. "Mrs. Lee and I will be having our wedding soon and you are all invited!" Kris announces to the guests. "What? Your fiance! No, I'm your fiance! You made a promise to me in fourth grade!" Courtney shouts, stomping her feet in anger. "Courtney, that was a long time ago, and I never promised anything. You assumed I said that." Kris responded in a calm voice. "No! I will not accept this! This ugly chick is not right for you!"

'Excuse me! What did she call me? Wait, his fiance?' My face burns and my head fills with confusion. Without a single thought in mind, I reach out and grab the collar of her dress, pulling her face close to mine. "Listen here, winch! I'm as good as you are, so shut your trap before I shut it for you!" Her eyes are wide with streaks of tears threatening to fall. I feel her tremble in fear. *'I guess nobody had the guts to stand up to her before!'* I begin to rec-

ollect my thoughts, getting my emotions under control. I see eyes staring in my direction, making me as pale as a ghost. I breathed in and slowly exhaled, pushing Courtney away from me, and letting her fall. "If you'll excuse me!" I say before running off through the maze, heading to the pond.

I sat on the swing feeling my eyes start to burn. I hear the whistle of the wind, the ripples in the water, and the songs of the birds in the trees. '*Being here is calming!*' "That stupid winch! Just wait! I'll be laughing in your face at me and Kris's wedding!" I shouted to the crystal blue sky. I feel my anger and sadness drift. Being sucked away by my surroundings. *'When did I want to marry him? My mind and I are not on the same track!'* As I sit, I look out to the clear water. I stood and walked closer. Hovering over the pond, I strip off my clothes one by one, then take one step forward. Instantly the cold water sends a chill up my spine. I head further in till the pond engulfs my body and soul, it feels like the pond is purifying me. Bathing in the water, droplets fall off my body as I raise my long thin fingers through my dripping wet hair.

"Robin!" A voice yelps. In a panic. I quickly plunge into the water, twisting and turning trying to search for the voice that has called out to me. Finally, seeing a bush move, I yelp and try to hurry out of the water. "Wait! It's me!" From the bushes, a body appears before me as well as arms that tangle around my body. "I've missed you!" The man moves his hands up to my face, pulling my head away from his broad shoulders. '*Jake!*' Tears of joy came forth. "Oh my gosh! Jack, I've missed you!" We hug for a while till a cold breeze brushes against my bare back. *'Oh crap!'* I pull back in a hurry, covering my body with my clothes, so nothing will be revealed. I hurry through a bush, throwing on my clothes, with my face burning in embarrassment.

Once the clothes are on I come out, but with twigs and leaves in my hair. I tried to brush them out with my fingers, but the more I did, the more tangled they got. "Let me help!" Jack comes close, reaching his hand to my head, and pulling out the twigs. "Thank you!" I say. I feel his big warm hand brush against my skin, making my heart leap out of my chest. "There!" He pulls back. "Ok, so shall we go?" He grabs my hand and yanks me a bit, but I pull back. "No! I'm sorry! I... I..." "She's my woman!" I hear Kris's voice boom and he pulls me into an embrace, his arms wrapped around my chest. I look up to his face, seeing his anger boil over. "That's what you say, but that's not what she wants!" Jack responds by grabbing and pulling my arm once more. *'This hurts!'* I wince in pain as my arm begins to feel like it's being pulled out of its socket and my neck feels like it's about to separate from my shoulders.

"Oh, Kris! Where are you?" Courtney's voice echoes from the maze. *'She's still here!'* I tried to pull out the guy's grip, but it only became tighter. "Both of you, let go!" I shouted in anger, but still, they glared at each other. "Found you, my love!" Courtney's voice chimes in as she comes around a bush. "My love?" Jack repeats, raising an eyebrow. "I thought you said Robin was your fiance, but it looks to me like that was a lie. So with this, I believe

I'll be taking Robin!" Jack yanks me away, loosening Kris's grip as Courtney pulls him back. "Oh! So she has a man! Then I have nothing to worry about!" She sings with a big grin. *'Ahh! She gets on my nerves!' Finally* able to use force, I shove Jack away and look him face to face. "I'm sorry Jack, but I said I wouldn't run away this time." With that I turned, grabbed Kris's face, and pulled it to mine, placing a deep kiss on his lips. I noticed that at first, he was shocked, but soon I could feel him kiss me back. My mind went blank, my legs started to become weak and my face began to burn. I started to drop to the ground, separating our lips, but Kris grabbed my waist supporting me, and kissed me deeper. This went on for a few minutes until blackness engulfed me.

"Mmm! What happened?" I sit up in bed and rub my head trying to thank what happened yesterday. After a bit of thinking, the memory came to me, making me blush. Quickly I pull the covers over my head, hands on my face, lightly touching my lips. *'I can't believe we did that in front of Jack and Courtney.'* Over and over Kris pops into my head, thinking of me and him kissing and the feeling it gave me. Tapping at the door brought me back to my surroundings and before I could pull the cover off it slowly creaked open. "Miss Robin, are you awake?" Melissa, my maid, calls my name then I can hear her footsteps walk around my bed, and with a sudden jerk of my cover, the cold air hits my body, then a bright beam hits me. "Up and Adams! It's going to be a busy day today!" The maid walks around pulling out clothes then goes to the bathroom turns on the water, and back to me. She yanks and tugs on my arm, getting me to the bathroom and stripping off my clothes. I get in the tub and from there she scrubs me down. Once done, she did my hair, makeup, and dressed me. Thank goodness she let me do some things on my own, I hate when others do things for me. Again, I'm being pulled, out the door, down the stairs, and into the dining room.

At the table I see Kris, wearing his big grin that takes over his face. "Good Morning!" He says. "Good morning master Kris!" The maid responds. I sat in a chair that she pulled out for me and started to eat the food, eggs, pancakes, and bacon, for the side, a glass of milk. "I trust you slept well?" Kris asks in a calm voice. "Yes, thank you for asking!" I stay quiet for a bit, till he speaks up once again. "Where would you like to go today?" I stop moving. *'Does he mean like on a date?'* "What do you mean?" "I was hoping we could go out today." He stands and heads my way then holds out his hand to me. "Sure!" I stand placing my hand on his and we head out to the car.

We get in, the car starts to move. I'm sitting right next to Kris, which makes me blush for what happened yesterday keeps replaying in my mind. It replays over and over. "You ok?" He asks, raising my head where I'm face to face with him. "I... I'm fine!" I smile, but he doesn't fall for it. He leans in. "Ok!" From there, his lips touch mine, lightly kissing me. It was not forced nor was it a deep kiss where I could barely breathe. "Where here master!" Rex announces from the small window that leads to the driver's seat. We get out, faced with the store that all women would dream to be in, Valentina La Rosa. In the store were many different kinds of dresses, frilly, professional, nightwear, party ones, or should I say clubbing. We go in and search for some dresses and then to another store. Through this day we jump to different buildings. Stores, the movies, and a cafe, we even stopped at a park and watched the sunset. The day felt long, but finally, it was close to an end, although Kris had one more place to go.

We step out of the car. Know face-to-face with one of the most expensive restaurants in Fort Worth, Horizon Palace. My eyes shine with delight. *'I always wanted to eat here!'* Inside I hear myself squeal in excitement. He leads me in, past tables and people. We soon stop in front of more doors. When open, two heads are bowed. "Welcome!" Kris nods his head and then leads me to a table. The room is empty, with only me and Kris, as well as some waiters setting out plates, drinks, and food. Throughout the room and on the table are candles along with soft romantic music. Next to our table is a window to the outside, greeting us, our reflection.

CHAPTER FIVE

Robin

"How is it?" Kris asks. "It's delicious!" I responded. What was ordered for me was French bread, Chicken Tikka Masala, for dessert was Mocha Pots De Crème, and to drink, Sparkling Raspberry Tea. It was a pleasure on my tongue. *'Heaven!'* Slowly, one bit after another. "Is it good?" I stopped mid-bite. I forgot all about Kris. I look at him with embarrassment. *'How can I eat like that in front of him!'* I pull out a mirror from my purse, to find crumbs around my lips and my lipstick smudged. I quickly grabbed my napkin and started to rub at the crumbs and my lipstick, but was stopped mid-way. A hand pulled mine away from my face. "Don't! You're going to make your face red and raw!" His face leans in closer to mine. I feel a tongue lick my lips before he pulls back. He stares me down with a silly grin on his face before his lips engulf mine. My head bends slightly back, his tongue wrapping around mine. I wrapped my arms around his head, tears threatening to come out. A slight moan slips through our lips.

"Mmmmm!" I feel his arms crawl over my body until he reaches my waist, pulling me out of my chair, then pushing my back up to the glass window. His heat, his scent, it all overcomes me. I feel myself starting to sway, my head becoming blank. My body burns and yearns for him to touch me more. His hands moved again, but down to the end of my dress. He tugs at the hem, pulling it slightly up. From there I snapped out of my trance, pushing him back. I tremble to realize what I have done. *'How can I do that when I love another, but wait! It's not wrong when I have feelings for him, right? But isn't that like two-timing? Ugg I'm so confused!'* My head spins trying to come up with a solution.

"Why do you always do that?" I jumped from this sudden outburst. "Wha... What do you mean?" "You always push me away whenever I try to embarrass you!" He huffs in anger, like a child who didn't get what they wanted. "I... I can't do this! I'm not ready!" "Ready for what? There's nothing you need to think about and just let me take control." I'm pushed up against the glass once more, his face closing in on mine. "So what you're saying is that you want me to be a lifeless puppet who you can control by the strings that I hang off of?" My lip quivers, my face turns red, and my eyes become watery. "Is that what you want because you don't seem to care how I feel about this matter? Heck! No one does!"

No movement! Kris stares at me in shock. "Robin! Not once-" "Stop! I don't want to hear it! Take me home!" From there, all was quiet. No words escaped mine, nor his lips. Once home we part ways. He heads wherever he goes and I head back to my room. Once inside I throw my bag on the ground and kick my shoes off my feet. I pulled out a chair from the small table, sat down then looked out of the window huffing in frustration. I watch the sun hide behind the earth that I am locked away from. If I could I would chase the sun to no end, going all over the world, just to escape this hell hole.

"Wakey! Wakey! Today is going to be a big day!" My body shakes as a squeaky voice sings in joy. I slowly sat up, but before I was able to do anything else, this overjoyed maid of mine yanked me like a rag doll. “Melissa, I'm tired! Can I please just lay in my bed for the rest of the day?” “Oh no dear, your wedding is today! We need to make you the most beautiful bride in the world, though that's not hard to do with your look!” She smiled at me as she dragged me around to the bathroom; undressed, scrubbed, and more, then back to my room where another maid was laying some clothes on my bed. Melissa rushes me as I reluctantly put on my clothes, a green shirt with light blue shorts and slippers, then down to the dining room where food is already set out. The day was like any other day, although it was rowdier with commotion; maids and butlers jumping from one room to another with decorations in their arms. Not only in the rooms and hallways, but in the kitchen. You can hear the clinging and clanging of dishes, and you can smell the aroma of different foods. In the yard, you can see people moving tables around and hearing the sound of the lawnmower.

I sit down at the table, plate ready like always. Today's breakfast was nothing special, just eggs, bacon, toast, and jelly, with a glass of milk. I began to eat, though the more I did the more I noticed that I was the only person at the table. "Where's Kris?" I asked Melissa. "He was called into work!" She responds, grabbing the plates and dishes that I have no use for anymore. *' He's been pestering me so much lately that I forgot he has a job!'* I sat there, a bit dumbfounded. "There's my baby girl!" I hear a woman cry out. I turn to face the person right as my hands grab my cheeks and squeeze them. "Hello, mother!" I say with squished cheeks. "Rose! You're going to ruin 'my' daughter-in-law's makeup!" Behind my mother, Rose, is my father, Daniel, and Kris's parents Mr. and Mrs. Preuett, Connor, and Jade.

Now with all the parents in the room, the woman on the couch, and the men by the bar, I stand in the middle of them, listening to their conversations. "This is so exciting!" I hear my mother squeal. My mother and Jade have been talking about after the wedding and where Kris and I should go for our honeymoon. At the bar, you could hear the men talking about a football game that seems to be coming on tonight and that they may have to pass on the wedding cake to go watch it.

"Milady!" Melissa walks into the room grabbing my hand. "I'm sorry for the sudden outburst, but I must hurry and get you ready." Once again, I was pulled by the arm to another room, with my mother and Mrs. Preuett caught on our tail. In the room was a mirror and chairs, as well as clothes hanging from every wear. Even so, there was one dress that caught my eye. The sleeveless milky white dress fell to my ankles in the back but cut off right above my knees in the front, and it had laces crawling down the sides. For the chest, it made a "v", so when I put it on it might show my cleavage. “Isn’t it beautiful!” Mrs. Preuett comes over standing right next to me. “It took him a long time to design this!” “Well, he has been planning this wedding since they were teenagers!” My mother chimes in. I looked at them with wide eyes, my cheeks flushed. *‘I have to admit, it's gorgeous!’* After a short while of me gawking at the dress, Melissa wastes no time rushing me into it. With it on I walk in front of the mirror and immediately notice it shows all my curves. Kris’s mother clapped in joy as my mother had tears falling from her eyes. “I can't believe my little girl is getting married!” She comes over, wrapping her arms around me and hugging me tightly. 'I've *always dreamed of wearing a wedding dress!'* Filled with delight, I forget everything around me. "Ok! I know you're enjoying yourself, but we still need to do your hair and makeup." Mrs. Preuett lightly grabs my mother's shoulders and helps her sit down before grabbing my wrist and setting me down in a chair right next to my mom. “She spins my chair around. "I'll do her makeup!" Mrs. Preuett says as my mother slides her hand into mine.

The makeover I received took around 40 minutes before I was dragged away to a pair of doors... The front door. Both my mother and Mrs. Preuett had left me right away when my hair was done, leaving me alone at the entrance. The next thing I know I hear the sound of music... Wedding music. *'Holy crap! We're having a wedding now!'* I stood there frozen solid. *'How did I not notice this? Why didn't anyone warn me? I thought I was just trying on the dress!'* Standing there, my mind scrambled with confusion, unable to move, on the verge of tears. "Ready!" My father walked up to me, grabbed my arm, then looked me in the face. "Sweetie, calm down! Everything will be ok!" From there, he lowers the veil over my face and retreats to his position as the doors open, uncovering the outside world.

I slowly walked down the aisle, terror growing more and more. As I do, an arm slides into mine. I look up to see my father, then look back out into the crowd. I feel the burning of eyes piercing my skin. I felt like I could almost die. I wanted to hurry and get to the end, but the closer I got, the more it seemed to distance itself. From there, I was on the verge of blacking out, and thanks to that feeling, without realizing it, I was next to Kris. "Dearly Beloved, we are gathered here today in the presence of these witnesses, to join Kris and Robin in matrimony..." I hear the preacher say these words before I begin to zone out, fear engulfing me. "I, Kris, take you, Robin..." I snapped back, hearing my name. "In sickness and in health, to love and to cherish; from this day forward until death do us part." I stood there, not knowing what to say or do. I started to panic. "Robin, calm down and just repeat what I say," Kris says, gripping my hand in his. He begins to whisper the vows and I try my best to repeat them. Now tears threatening my eyes I spit out the vowels. "I... I, Rob... Robin, take you Kri... Kris, to be my husband, too... to have and to... to hold from this day forward, for... for better or for... for worse, for richer, for... for poorer, in sickness and... and in health, to love and to... to cherish; from this day forward unt... until death do we par... part." My legs begin to give and I almost fall after I say the last word, and now realize all my energy is gone. Luckily Kris caught me. "I, Kris, give you, Robin, this ring as an eternal symbol of my love and commitment to you. As for you, Robin, give me, Kris, this ring as an eternal symbol of our love and commitment to me." Kris announces this for me, knowing I was unable to say anything more. Once again the preacher's voice booms to the crowd, "By the power vested in me by the State of Texas, I now pronounce you husband and wife. You may now kiss the bri-" "Stop! I object to this wedding! That woman belongs to me!"

I look over and down the aisle to see Jack pointing a gun toward us. "Jack! What are you doing?" I hear Mrs. Phinks voice screech in fear as she stands in the crowd. "Shut up, mother! This has nothing to do with you!" Jack screams back. "Give me back Robin!" Now able to stand from the adrenaline of fear, I took one foot forward before being pulled back and behind Kris. "Stupid! Are you still trying to leave me?" Kris says, sadness combined in his voice. "No I-" "Kris! You told me if I wanted Robin back I had to kill you. Well, I'll do just that!" I grab Kris shoving him to the side at the sound of a gun going off. The next thing I know pain strikes me from my side and I'm falling to the ground. "Robin!" Multiple voices scream out my name and a pair of arms are wrapped around my limp body. "Robin! Don't leave me!" Kris says, squeezing me, tears falling from his eyes. I look down at my dress, seeing it has been drenched in blood, losing its beautiful milky white color. I look back at Kris with a big grin. "The dress is ruined! I'm sorry!" "Don't say that! The dress doesn't matter!" I raise a hand to his face, caressing it, and wiping the tears. After a couple of seconds, I open my mouth, letting go of my last breath, "I love you!"

CHAPTER SIX

Robin

The bleary darkness punctuated by rhythmic beeping with a harsh light that beckoned my consciousness back to the surface. As I'm coming to, I can hear the soft whimpers near me along with the feeling of gentle hands caressing my right cheek. Now as I endeavor to open my weak eyes, through the haze I see a figure moving closer. Suddenly the figure yells, bringing me fully out of my stupor. "Robin!" Only then do I realize it's my mother. Grabbing at her clothing I feel the heavy weight that is my body trying to move. Tears slip past my deprived eyes as she pulls me into a hug so tight I can hardly breath.

'Thank you Lord... Wait! What happened to Jack?' I pulled my head away from my mother, whipping away the tears in horror. "Mother, where is Jack? How is he?" Her tears slow down as she looks away in disgust. "Mother! Please tell me!" I look at her

with big eyes full of fear for his life. "He..." My mother stopped and looked me straight in the face. "He's none of your concern! Rest, you still aren't well." She stands and tries to walk away, but my grasp on her clothing tightens. "No, mother! Please... I need to know!" More tears threatened to spill out as I looked down at my sheet. "Please! Just tell me he's ok!" I hear her let out a deep sigh before she sits back next to me grabbing the hand that has a hold of her. "Sweetie! He's in jail for attempted murder." "Is... Is there anything I can do? I'm not angry about his actions. On the contrary, I sympathize with him." My mother stands once again, grabbing my shoulders in terror at my words. "Why? Why do you say that after he shot you!" I look at her with a serious expression. "Mother! I loved Jack and I will always care for him, but one thing I know. If it wasn't for that day! The day I ran away from this house! He would have never been in this situation in the first place. I am the source of his actions. So for that, I will not press charges." Her arms drop to her side. Not one word came out of her lips for she knows once I make a decision, I'll stick with it. "Fine! Do as you wish. The only thing I want from you is to marry Kris. From there, live your life the way you want to." My mother kissed me on my head before she left the room. After that, a nurse came in and told me that I have been asleep for six weeks and that I fully recovered, so I was released from the hospital. I just need to be careful and I will have a scar due to the wound.

Walking up the steps to the mansion that started it all. It's everything that I can't turn my back on. As I walk on, memories flow through my head. The first time I met Kris was when we were kids. The time when in middle school he would bully me and ignore me. In high school, where he hangs all over me. To everything that led to this moment. I reach for the doors of the home that belongs to my love. Slowly the doors creak open. One step after another, the sound echoes throughout the home. I walked down the hall and up the steps to the door with a nameplate on it that read "Kris Preuett's study". I twisted the knob and cracked it open to where I was able to squeeze my head through. My eyes widened in horror. *'What happened!'* Trash, books, and paper were thrown all over the floor, pictures on either side were cracked, and his desk flipped over. I slowly stepped in, my eyes attached to the office chair that faced his shattered window, the chair was the only thing untouched. I walked up and then around it to find a sleeping man... Kris.

Seeing him for the first time after I was shot was all I wanted, but this state he was in shattered my heart. His short brown hair was all messy along with his clothes disheveled and ruined. I reached my hand up to his cheek to find the touch cold as ice. My hands slide past his cheeks and around his head, my arms wrapping around his neck longing for his touch after everything. My face up to his, I kiss his lips and then lean into his ear. "Rise and shine my love!" I noticed his eyes flutter open at the sound of my voice and felt his arms grabbing my waist. "You're alive!" He shouts as he holds me tight, his face buried in my stomach. He looked like a child who lost everything.

I felt a sharp pain in my right foot from standing here for what felt like forever, so I shifted on my feet feeling the strain fade away. When I moved I felt his grip around me tighten, and without a word I was swept up off my feet, feeling his strong arms wrap around me. I quickly grab on to his shirt as he rushes us out the door and straight into his room. Staring into the pitch black room I squirm a bit. “Hey Kris, can you put me down or turn on the light?” He said nothing. I look up at him, my eyes begging to adjust to the darkness, I notice him looking down at me. After kicking the door shut, he walked us to the bed then gently laid me down on my back before crawling on top of me. I feel Kris slide my hair away from my neck as he leans in, his hot breath touches my skin, sending chills down my spin. His lips touched mine, but at first it was only the tip of his soft lip. Slowly he devoured me, my lips parting just a bit for him to slip his tongue in. I then started to feel his strong hands crawling up my stomach, his thumb lightly brushing across my scar before moving to my breast as the other slid under my jeans. I felt his hands massage the places that they were in contact with. A light moan slipped past my lips making him grin into the kiss. His lips parted from mine, sliding down to my neck tracing kisses in every spot. This feeling was ecstasy.

My body yearns for his touch. He threw off his clothes after he slowly lifted off my shirt before laying me down and unbuttoning my pants before taking them off along with my underwear and laying on top of me once again. Now feeling his warm skin on mine, I slide my fingers down his chest, feeling ever abe as he fondles my nipples with his tongue, his fingers teasing my clit. A moan again slips through my lips once more in pleasure. “You're so wet!” He says, raising his face to mine. “Please! Don’t tease me anymore!” I squirm under him. “ Please! Put it inside me!” I feel his hand move down to my waist, his shaft teasing my entrance. I wiggle my hips a bit as my legs wrap around his waist trying to pull him closer. He slowly slid the tip in first, inching it further and further inside me. The more he was in me the more pain I could feel from him taking my virginity. Tears push past my eyes as my nails begin to dig into his back. “Does it hurt?” He looks down at me with worried eyes. I smile and lick his lips. "I'm fine!" He pushes in a bit further, trying his best not to hurt me. After a few seconds I took a deep breath, slowly releasing it I spoke, “It's ok, you can move faster!” He lightly nods then picks up his past. Thrusting in and out of me, the pain easing, slowly becoming pleasurable. My arms around him tighten as he slams deep inside me. I began moaning louder and louder, “Kris!” “Oh Robin, I love you!” He whispers into my ear before kissing me and I could feel something warm inside my womb.

Light poured into the room past the black curtains hitting my face causing me to wake from my slumber. Scrunching my brows, I tried to turn away from the window but the arms that were tightly wrapped around me held me in my place. I can feel his light breathing against my ear as he moves closer to me, his face nuzzling into my hair as his legs entwined with mine. I felt engulfed by his body that I fell back to sleep without realizing.

"Robin! It's time we get up!" Dazed, I slowly sit up yawning but from a sharp pain I'm hunching over with my arms wrapped around myself. *'Ahh why does my wait hurt so much and when did I fall back to sleep?'* Kris stands over me, dressed in nothing but his tight boxers, I stare at him as he leans over placing a hand on my back. “Are you ok? Do you need anything?” Entranced by him and his hot body I shake my head aggressively. “I'm ok, but... um, do you mind if we eat in bed today?” He nods, “Sure, but while you wait would you like to take a bath? I have it running for you!" He replies as he places a kiss on my head. “I would love that!” Smiling, I leaned on him as his hands slid under me then was picked up off the bed. “Hehe, I can walk!” “Let me take care of you, I know you must be a bit sore!” Gently he places me in the tub, warm water consuming my body, easing the pain from last night. “I'm going to get your food, take as long as you need dear!” He kisses my lips before leaving me alone. After awhile I get out of the bath, wrapping a towel around me, I walk over to the closet forgetting I don’t have anything to wear here. I walk over to Kris’s closet, finding one of his black shirts. I slip it on, the heavy shirt falling past my hips. *‘Hehe! Who would ever think I would be wearing one of Kris Preuett’s shirts and that I, Robin Lee would be with him!’* Gripping his shirt, I pull it over my face taking in a deep breath getting lost in his scent. “Enjoying yourself?” I jump as his arms wrap around me from behind. “Last night was wonderful!" I hear Kris whisper in my ear before he walks me out of his closet. Blushing, I tilted my head back looking up at him. “So what's there to eat?” I asked, changing the subject. We walked over to the table in his room. He pulls out the chair then sits down before picking me up and setting me on his lap. “Today they made you brunch; pancakes, eggs, and bacon with a glass of orange juice.” I look at the two plates in front of me. “How will you eat with me on your lap?” I ask him as he nuzzles his face into my neck. “I can wait!”

Shakingly, I take my last bite of eggs. I look back down at the empty dishes laying down my fork then shift on his lap, my nerves growing more and more. *'I can feel his hard dick throbbing under me for a while now!'* Noticing my movement, his hands grasp my waist, keeping me firmly against his bulge. "Do you feel better?" He asks as a hand slides up my neck, and uses the back of his hand to slide my hair away, giving him access to my bare skin. He then traces light kisses on me. "I'm... I'm feeling much better!" I reply mumbling under my breath, my lips quivering along with the feeling of my heart speeding up from his touch. His other hand strayed from my side trailing to my inner thigh, gripping it tightly. The heat rises to my cheeks as his grasp on me forces me to lean back on his chest. Noticing my dilemma, a sly smirk grew across his face before he forced my legs apart before gently tracing the tips of his fingers from my thighs to my sex, his thumb stopping right over my clit. "Are you feeling any pain here, hun?" I can feel myself melting from his touch, slowly losing my train of thought as I faintly shake my head. His fingers slip through my lips allowing them to thrust in and out, his fingers soaked from my juices. "K...Kris!" I get out from under my breath, trying to get a grasp on my mind, only to fail as he pushes his fingers inside me harder. "Ahhh I want you!" I moan tugging on the shirt I wore. "Good girl!" It's like a guttural call to my soul. He then lifts me up aiming his hard rod before shoving it deep into my pussy. I quiver, my nails digging into his arms as he raises me then slams me back down on him pushing deeper. "How's that feel hun?" He asks as he twitches his cock inside my womb. "I... I want more!" I rock my waist, giving up on a sane mind, letting my lust for this man consume me. He releases my legs and nuzzles his face into my neck, grazing his teeth against my skin, as his hands slide under my shirt and over my tits. With my nipples between his fingers, my breasts firmly fitting into his large hand, he begins to squeeze, pinch and pull. “Show me how bad you want me!” I began to bounce faster on his member as it slid deeper and faster, wanting every bit of him inside me. “Kris, it feels so good deep inside me!” He growls against my neck biting a bit harder causing me to slam down on him, moaning loudly to where the whole house could possibly hear. He quickly covers my mouth as he pushes harder inside as he shoves me down on his desk as he now towers over me, my breast squished.

"Master Kris and Lady Robin?” Rex knocks on the door. My cheeks flushed and I began to grab at Kris’s arm. *‘Oh, my God! Did Rex hear me? Oh my god!’* I tried to get him to stop but his hold on me was too strong, his hand up the shirt pressing firmly on my bare back. “Sir, I just wanted to let you know your car is ready and I have Malissa out here with the set of clothes you asked for!” “Kris… Please!” I whisper through a repressed moan as I feel him pulsing inside me. “Just a bit more love!” He thrust deeper inside me, my eyes rolled back. “I want to cum deep inside you!” I bite down on my bottom lip, but he slides a finger in between my lips. “Don't do that, you're going to damage your lips!” His finger rubs against my lips as he thrusts one last time inside me. His cum feeling me as I cum with this man, though I may have came more than that. I breathe exhausted as he picks me up and lays me back on the bed before opening the door a bit and taking his clothes. “We will be down in a bit!” He says before shutting the door.

As we walked downstairs to the front door, I shot him a death glare. I had to take another shower so it took us a bit longer to leave the room. “You look beautiful in blue!” He glanced down at my knee-high dark blue dress. I look forward and close my eyes. “Well, I look good in everything!” I reply with a smirk. Suddenly he grabs my arm pulling me to him, his lips peck mine. “Of course you do!” I blush and yank my arm from him, rushing to the car, I hear him chuckling behind me. I swing the door open and get in the car, shutting the door behind me and then locking it. I look out the window sticking out my tongue to him. He then walks to the other side of the car. *‘Shoot! I forgot the other door!’* I tried to crawl to the other side, but it was too slow. I almost fell out of the car due to him opening it. He grabs me, moves me over, and sits next to me. “Heh, you need to be more careful!” I sit there looking down pouting, arms resting on my lap as the car moves forward.

"Umm..." I look up at Kris, hands pulling at my dress. *'I wonder if he would mind if I ask to go see Jake and to release him from prison?'* Worried to ask, I gazed out the window of the car. "What is it?" I feel his hand grab mine as another wraps around my waist, pulling me closer, and my heart rate rises. "Is... Is it ok if we go visit Jake and liberate him?" I finally spit out, giving him my puppy eyes and a quivering lip. "What? Why would you want to do that after he shot you?" His hands turn cold. "It's not like he wanted to shoot me, plus it's my fault! If I didn't run away! If I had gone through with the engagement then none of this would have happened to him!" I grip his hand, nails penetrating his skin. "I'm sorry, but I can't do that!" My teeth grind together in anger. "Stop the car!" I screech, then feel the car jerk. I unbuckle and swing open the door, putting one foot out before my arm is pulled. "Where are you going?" He crushes my wrist, fury shows on his face. "I'm going to bail Jake out of jail!" Slowly the anger he showed died for he knows I won't give this up. "Fine, but I don't want you to be by yourself in the same room as him and I don't want him touching you! Also, I have a condition if we release him!" "What are the conditions?" I ask him, tilting my head to the side. "Just one, I'm putting a restraining order on him and you'll never see him again!" *'Ok, that's fair! I just don't want to ruin his life and his poor mother! I put her through so much and he's all she has!'* I smile at him. "I agree with your condition!" I notice his eyes soften. I slide back into the car and lean into his cheek, kissing it. "Thank you!"

As we walk down the hall, a police officer leads us to Jake's jail cell. I clutch at Kris's arm a little scared of the ones behind the bars, staring at us intensely, some yelling, cursing, and some whistling at me as we walk on. We walked a few ways till he opened one. "Jake Phinks!" The officer shouts and once he does, I see a tall black-haired man step out. "Jake!" I squeal, lunging at him and wrapping my arms around him. "Robin! Is it really you? I thought I killed you!" He hugs me, squeezing me for dear life. "No, I'm alive!" "Excuse me!" Next thing I know I'm being pulled away from Jake's embrace and slung over Kris's shoulder. *'Crap! The promise!'* "Yes, this is all fine and dandy, but we have somewhere to be, and you need to apologize to your mother!" He says, turning and taking a few steps. "What do you mean?" I struggled to look up at Jake and to find a confused look on his face. "My sweet darling here forgave you for your actions and we came to release you!" From there the floor starts to move and I can see the police officer, with Jake at hand, following us, but only to the entrance of the building.

He shoved me into the car, forcing me to lie on my back. He gets in, slamming the door behind him before placing his hands on either side of me, his head looking down at me. "You broke your promise!" A dark aura surrounds him. He leans closer to my face allowing me to see his eyes turn dark, almost fully black. "How should I punish you?" As he says this, I feel a hand move from my arm, down my stomach, all the way to the hem of my dress. He slides his hand under, his fingers rubbing me through my underwear. I blush in embarrassment with a moan slipping past my lips. I wanted more! Rocking my hips I was getting lost in this pleaser but midway feeling my climax, he suddenly stopped. "I can't let you finish now can I? How should I punish you!" I squirm under him, face burning, my breathing becoming heavy. He sits up, moving back to his seat. I feel distressed by the desire he made rise inside me.

I sit up looking at him with a dejected expression. Nothing! He just looks out the window, saying nothing. After a good while of silence, the driver finally speaks up when he slides open the little window between us and him. "Sir, we're here!" Before getting out or giving me a chance to look out the window, Kris ties his necktie over my eyes, blinding me. I feel my body rise and my face is shoved into a chest, then there's movement. No words are spoken, I can just hear doors and footsteps. "Know then!" He had sat me down on something soft and squishy. With concern, I raise my hand to the tie that is blinding me, but my hands were stopped by hard big ones. "No! Leave it on!" *'What's going on?'* While blind, I feel my dress rise over my head then my shoes sliding off my feet, leaving me in only my underwear. I quickly tried once more to tear off the tie but my face was shoved into the cushion. I reach my hand out gripping his shirt but he grabs my wrist pulling it behind my back then he grabs my other hand. Soon I begin to hear something rattle and feel something cold against my skin. *'A chain?'* "Stay still!" I hear Kris say as he begins to cuff my wrists, connecting them together. "That's a good girl!" I feel my heartbeat speed up. "Kri... Kris! What are you doing?" I try to sit up, but his arms keep me down "Didn't I say I would punish you?" After that, I feel him move away from me, taking his warmth with him. “Kris, I said I was sorry!” Finally free I shoot up and slide my legs off the edge of what I'm assuming is a bed and place my bare feet on the hard, cold floor. I walk forward, swaying a bit. “Kris? Are you there?” It's quiet. No sound but my own. Tears stream down my cheeks as realization begins to set in. *‘Is this his idea of punishment? Was a hug really that bad? Is he just going to leave me like this alone in a room?’* Questions run through my head and my legs give up on me forcing me to slide onto the floor. I sit there, my lips quivering.

Arms cuffed behind my back, striped on a cold floor, in a room I believe to be all alone. The touch in the car still lingers on my skin. *‘With me sitting here crying, why am I still aroused!’* Right now I’m a mess with puffy eyes as well as a dog in heat, waiting to be slammed. My breathing gets heavy as I squeeze my legs together wishing I was able to satisfy this desire. "Kris... Kris, I'm sorry I broke the promise, but is this really called for?" I call out, but only hear echoes of my own voice. *'He acts just like a child!'* I fidget on the floor trying to think of a way for him to forgive me and stop me from hurting. I lay down on my back, crushing my hands. I wince in pain but try to ignore it. I lay there for a good while, not moving one bit. "Forget it, I apologized and felt bad for breaking our promise, but you're taking this too far. So if you're just going to keep me like this I'm just going to stay right here on the cold floor, crushing my hands and if I get sick, it's on you. Also, I'm rethinking our relationship at this point!" I start to hear stomping in the room. *'Asshole! You have the nerve to arouse me then tie me up and watch me in agony!'* "When I get out of this I'm going to the police for a restraining order. I don't want you anywhere-" "I swear if you finish that god damn sentence!" He picks me up off the floor and lays me back on the bed. "Leave me alone! I'm done! I'm not going to go through this due to your pettiness!" His hands grab onto my chin pulling my face up. "You are my woman! No one is allowed to touch you or ever take you from me!" He bites my bottom lip. "I get I can be immature and can take things too far, but don't ever threaten me with our relationship. After last night, you are mine forever!" He kissed my lips, his tongue sliding into my mouth wrapping around mine. "Mmmh!" I moaned against the kiss, though before I knew it he was flipping me back on my stomach racing my butt up to him. Hearing a zipper and ruffling of his jeans, it wasn't long till I felt his little companion start to rub up against my damp panties. I pushed my waist back as my mind became fuzzy with the desire, images of his naked figure flooding my brain. He places his hands on my ass, sliding his thumbs under what little clothes I had on. He pulls the thin fabric a side allowing my juices to slide down my thighs. “My poor baby!” He says under his breath as his fingers gently caress my clit before he slides a finger inside. I bit down on my bottom lip feeling it go in and out but it was not enough. “I want more!” I grabbed the sheets as I leaned down, raising my hips higher. I can hear rustling on the bed before the tip of his cock rubbing against my slit. A hand grasps my wrist as he leans over my back, his lips right next to my ear. “I love you, Robin! And I'm sorry for putting you through so much!” I can hear the guilt behind his words.. “Kris, I love you and I really want you!” He slams inside me. “You mean everything to me!” He grunts as he thrust inside me again. I bite down on the sheets as he licks my neck. He thrust harder and faster keeping a steady paste, I can feel my nipples becoming raw as they rub against the fabric. “Kris, I want it inside me!” I moan out feeling my climax approaching. “Robin!” He moans as his warm cum feels my inside.

I don't know how many times we did it in the room, but again I passed out. Eyes fluttering open, light seeps through. The tie that covered my eyes has now been removed along with the heavy metal that was on my wrists, leaving red marks on my skin. Dazed by the mark I jump when a sudden pair of arms wrap around my waist and a face is buried into my neck. I raised a hand to brush Kris's hair but was stopped when there was a knock on the door. Kris moves his head off of me shouting, "Yes?" "Master Kris, lady Robin, I have brought you a pair of clothes, and the car is ready to send you home. I feel the bed rise as Kris stands up and heads over to the door. *'Wait! Where are we!'* I sit up and look around the unfamiliar room. “Kris, where is this?” “It's a hotel milady!” I hear Rex respond when Kris cracks the door, grabbing our clothes. He walks back over handing me a pair, then he heads off to the bathroom. Once he finished showering and getting dressed, I got up and did the same.

I sit in the car, my head in a bit of a daze from last night. “Would you like to go out to eat or is there anywhere specific you'd like to go?” I look out the window, watching buildings go by. “Mmm! What about bagels?” My mouth watered a bit as my stomach grumbled! *‘Mmm, a blueberry cream cheese bagel sounds so good right now!’* I can hear Kris chuckle as he licks my lips, snapping me from my daze. “Anything for you love!” He says as he knocks on the sliding door. He leans into it and tells the driver to find the closest bagel shop. He then leans back into his seat looking down at my wrists that are laid on top of my lap. “He grabs my hands and pulls my wrists close to his lips, lightly kissing them. “I’m sorry dear!” I see his eyes soften. I lean in and peck his lips.

On the way, home I’m nibbling on my bagel in enjoyment. Kris taps on his phone, doing work or something. It doesn’t take long till we get home and he quickly gets out of the car, helps me then rushes us into the house. “Love I have work I need to finish, so I'll be in my office if you need me.” He kisses me before heading to his office and shutting the door behind him. Looking around I only had one thing on my mind, *‘I just want to go back to sleep!’* I rush upstairs and straight into my room stripping off my clothes before falling onto the bed and snuggling into the sheets. *‘It still smells like him!'* My eyes close as I slowly drift into slumber. A loud clacking sound echoed throughout the room, making me jump, my heart racing from the sudden sound from the window. Click Clack! Again, clicking comes from the window. I stand wrapping the sheets around my bare skin and head to the window, opening the curtains. Down on the first floor was a man with red hair. *'Do I know him?'* I stand there, staring at the man who is now waving and signaling. Then it hit me. *'Oh, my god! Derick!'* I run back to the bed, grab my clothes, and try to shove them on before running out the door and down the steps. "Please let me in, I need to see Robin." I hear his voice echo in the halls, coming from the entrance. Once down the steps, I yell his name, jumping into his arms. I look up into his brown eyes. "You've gotten so big, how have you been?" Derick picks me up, holding onto me. "I'm ok, what about you?" "Better after finally seeing you." "When did you get here and how did you know where I was." "I just arrived today and I called your parents." He walked into the house, one conversation to another. How he's been, what he has done and I told him Somethings too. "Wait, you're married?" "No, I got shot which canceled the wedding." "But you do have a fiancée?" He asked. "Yes!" Derick looks at me with shock. "Is that an issue?" I look up to see Kris. *'Ahhh! Not good!'* I tape Derick telling him to put me down, but he doesn't. I tap on him again. He does nothing. "I won't accept this!" He looks at me. "What did your parents say?" "Uh... Um... They-" "They allowed it, I mean they did arrange this since she was a child." Kris cuts me off. "Then that makes all the difference. Robin, you're coming with me back to Frances." He starts back to the entrance of the door, but it is slammed shut by Rex. "Move!" Derick's face seems to darken with anger. "I'm sorry sir, but I only take orders from master Kris." He stands there.

"Fine, then I'll just stay here. You! Maid, show me to my room!" He slowly put back down on the ground. Derick follows the maid and Kris grabs onto me, embracing me. Once gone, his hands grip my shoulders, he leans down and looks me in the eyes. "Who is he?"

CHAPTER SEVEN

Robin

'Derick's been an old friend since I was little. He is four years older than me; which means he is twenty-six now. Back then, when we last saw each other, I was seven and he was eleven. We would always play together and when Kris came around, I would hide Derick. So ya they have never met before. One day when Kris was camping with his family, Derick was at my house playing dolls with me. As we were having fun, his mother barged in, grabbing him by the arm and dragging him off. I followed them out, just to find a truck and things being shoved inside. "What's going on?" I rushed up to Derick and his mother. "We are moving to France, so hurry up and say your goodbyes." Then she walked off. "Are you staying here?" I look up at him, staring into his brown eyes. He closes them, then shakes his head no. I can barely remember what happened next, but I do remember tears sprouting out of my eyes and gripping at him begging him not to go. After that, I was left with Kris and nobody else.'

"Well... He's an old friend from when we were kids!" "Then how come I'm just now learning about him? I mean, we have been together ever since we were little." Looking into his blue eyes, confusion takes over. "Um... Well... I... I kind of hid him from you." I look down at my feet. "What? Why? How?" I look back up at him, a bit frustrated. "Because you always get rid of my friends. You would always scare them off or threaten them!" I shouted, throwing my hands in the air. "He was the only one I couldn't let you take away from me." From confusion to guilt. "I'm sorry! I wanted you all to myself and I was afraid of losing you to another guy." He grips my hands, wrapping them around his neck before wrapping his around my waist. "You know how I feel for you, and those feelings will never change." He lightly kisses my cheek. From my cheek to forehead, to my eyelids, then pecking my lips. He looks at me before devouring my mouth. "What are you doing?" Lips parting, I feel the collar of my dress getting pulled from behind forcing me to fall on a solid figure... Human. I look up to see who it is and to find Derick. Without a word he picks me up, swinging me on his hip like I'm luggage, then walks off. Mind blank, I dangle there on his side, staring at the ground.

Dizzy from the blood draining to my head, I don't notice we arrive at a house. *'When did we get outside?'* "Yes! May I help you?" I hear Charlie's voice, my parent's butler. "I would like to speak to Mr. and Mrs. Lee, please!" Derick says, setting me on my feet and grabbing my hand. "Right this way!" Charlie says, opening the door further before leading the way. We walked down the hall and to the back door. Charlie opened it. Through the door, I see a pool and my father splashing around in it. As for my mother, she's under an umbrella, laying down, maids waiting for her hand and foot. Before we went out to them, Derick clutched my hand tighter. "Mr. and Mrs. Lee, please excuse my intrusion!" He marches up to the pool, yanking me behind him. "Derick!" My mother yelps, standing and embracing him. "It's been so long! How are you? You've grown so much! Oh, is your parent here? I heard you have a new sister, how is she? Is she here?" Constantly my mother babbled, not letting Derick spit out a word. "Mrs. Lee, let's talk about this later, right now I have something very important to confirm about."

"Ok! Come, come! What is it you are wishing to talk about?" Wrapping herself in a towel, she leads us back inside to the living room. We sat down, she in her recliner and us sitting on the couch. "I would like to take Robin's hand in marriage." She stops rocking in her chair and stares at him, speechless. As for me, I turned to stone. *'Did I hear that right?'* "Come again?" My mother says. "I would like to take your daughter's hand in marriage," Derick repeats. I see my mother's smile fade, and I know why. "No can do!" She stands and starts walking off, but Derick rushes in front of her, not letting her pass. "Why? I know you gave your daughter away and for that kind of love, it will never be content." I slowly walk up, grabbing his shoulder. "What do you know?" I feel tears spring into my eyes. "How on earth would you know that our love isn't real?" I shouted from the top of my lungs. *'What am I saying? Why am I crying? Why do his words hurt?'* "Of course, you would not know, I hid you from Kris hoping you would stay by my side, but you left me. You went overseas and have not communicated with me since, so who are you to say my relationship won't last? You especially have nothing to say for you have no idea what I have been through." I look up at him, breathless. His face shows a hurt expression

Standing there, he grabs my hands. "You're missing the main point of this! I'm sorry I said something to hurt you, but Robin, I want you. I came back for you! Throughout these fifteen years, you have always been on my mind. I have tried to get in contact with you, but my parents have been stopping me from any contact with you, so to be able to be together with you once again, I stayed there until I gained my father's business." He pulls me into his chest, wrapping his arms around my waist. "I love you Robin and I have for a long time. Are you just going to ignore my feelings for you?" "Why should she care!" At the entrance of the room, Kris appears. He walks up to me and Derick, grasping my wrist and yanking on it, but Derick denies letting go and grabs my wrist as well, tugging. *'Why does it feel like I've been through this before!'* My tears dry up, going from sadness to annoyance. The two men argue and jerk on my arms. "Ok! I think that's enough." My mother announces, pulling me away from the two men. Even so, they still ram their heads at each other. My mother tries again, but they are too into an argument. Next thing I know, my father walks in, slamming Kris's and Derick's heads together. I flinched from hearing the loud crash and instantly hurried to Krise's aid. I look at Derick, and he stares back with a heated expression.

I look back at Kris, a wave of sadness overflows me, but not one tear dares to slip past. Once Kris is ok, we loop arms and turn away. "We are heading back. I'm sorry to disturb you, mother! Father!" Then we head out, down the hall to the entrance of the home, then out to the front yard. "Robin! Wait!" Derick's voice shouts from behind. I ignore him and keep walking, but he grabs my shoulder, slightly turning me. "What I said! I really mean it. I've been in love with you. Please think about it!" He slowly turns and heads back to my parent's home.

I sat Kris in his office chair, kneeling at his feet and rubbing his head. "Are you ok?" I ask. "I'm ok, don't worry!" He grabs me, lifting me onto his desk. He snuggles his face into my stomach, arms wrapped around my waist. I brush my fingers through his hair. As we sat there, my tears began to flow. *'In the end, I lost another friend because of you Kris!'* I stare at the back of his head, tears falling onto his hair. *'Even so, I love you! Please don't ever leave me!'* I feel a hand raise up my spine up to the back of my neck, then notice him staring at me. He raises another hand, but up to my cheek, and wipes away my tears. "What's wrong?" I shake my head, a smile crossing my face. "Nothing!" I cup his face, raising his to mine, then kiss his lips. "I love you, Kris!"

I see happiness rise in Kris's eyes. "Robin!" He leans in for another kiss, but I put my hand up to his chest, stopping him. "But even though I love you, I feel I need time to think about all that has happened. I understand everything we have been through, this... What we have should be love, but I feel the words that I just spoke could be something else." "What?" Kris sits up from my words, eyes wide. "How? How could you say that?" I feel my lips quiver. "Does this mean you're considering his feelings? Are you planning on leaving me for him?" He stands. "What... What if I am?" "Why do you say this to me, the one you've been with for years? Robin, you say you don't know if our relationship is love, but I know it is. You know, does your heart quiver when he says your name, do you shiver when you feel his touch, do you get aroused from just hearing 'I love you' from his voice? Well, you know, I see your reaction when I do it." He grips my wrist, pushing my back against his desk. "Robin!" *'Yes, my heart quivers from hearing my name slip past your lips.'* "See! I can hear your heart beating for me." He slides a hand down my chest, forcing me to close my eyes. *'Yes, I shiver from only a touch from you!'* "I can see goosebumps cover your arm, from a single touch from me." He says this. As he cherishes me I hear a whisper next to my ear. "I love you!" From that, I squirm under him, biting my bottom lip. *'Yes... Yes, I feel all stirred up from hearing those words from you!'* "That's how! That right there is how I know you and I are in love."

"Kris!" I moan his name as his hand pulls up my dress, then starts sliding his hand over my leg as the other grips my breast through the cloth. The more I feel him caress me the more my desire grows. My head becomes foggy. I jump when I hear a knock at the door. Irritated, Kris sits up, fixing his shirt, then helps me stand. "Come in!" I hear him shout as I try to fix my tangled hair. The door opens revealing Rex and a little girl next to him. She jumps in and runs to me. "Oh my goodness! Oh my goodness! I have been dying to meet you! My brother talks a lot about you!" I stare at her, as she jumps around in a circle. *'Her brother? Hmmm! Red hair, brown eyes. Does she mean...'* I knelt down to the girl. "Are you Derik's little sister?" She smiles brightly and puts her hands behind her back. "Yep! My name is June and I'm eight years old." She announces as she rocks on her feet. "Well June, I'm Robin. Nice to meet you." She throws a hand forward and shakes mine. "June, are you here by yourself?" Once I say that she pouts. "Ya! My brother told me not to come, but I really really wanted to meet you!" "Where are your parents?" I stand. "They went back to France!" "Then who's watching you?" "My brother!"

"June! Are you here?" I hear Derick's voice echo in the house. I see June jump, then run behind me as Derik enters Kris's office. "Why did you run off?" Derick walks up to me and crouches down. "I'm sorry! I just..." June grips my dress. "I just really wanted to meet Robin!" I see tears slip past her eyes. Derick lets out a big sigh. "Ok, I understand. Now come here!" She walks around me and jumps into her brother's arms. He stands with June at hand, looking at me with a slight grin. "I'm sorry she intruded!" I grabbed June's hand, smiling. "It's ok! I would love it if you came again June and next time we can have a playdate." She smiles brightly, wiping away her tears. "Mm!" She then puts up her pinky. "It's a promise?" I put mine up to hers, entwining them. "It's a promise!" I step back, feeling Kris wrapping an arm around my waist. "Well, we better get going," Derick announces. "I'll walk you out." I brushed off Kris's hand and left him in the office. I headed out with them to the front door, then watched them leave.

Once gone, I walked back to Kris's office, but he wasn't there. I walked out and started searching the rooms throughout the house, but he was nowhere to be found. As I wander around, looking for Kris, I enter the kitchen. There Rex, Aaron, and Finn chatted with each other. *'I haven't seen them in a while.'* I walk up to them, gripping Aaron, who's back faces me. "Miss!" Aaron and Finn speak together. "Nice to see you, Miss Robin." Rex bows to me. "Hey, have yall seen Kris?" Rex approaches me and leans next to my ear. "Have you checked the pond?" *'Ahh! I didn't think of that!'* I turn and head to the pond.

Once through the garden, I spot a man swinging on the swing. I walk up, wrapping my arms around his neck. "What's wrong?" No answer! He just sits there looking out at the scenery. Hands on his chest, I feel it rise from every breath he takes. I slid my face down to his cheek, brushing my lips against him. No reaction! Now irritated, I breathe in and hold it in my cheeks, standing up straight. *'Ahhh! What's his deal? He could at least acknowledge me!'* I stormed around him, now face to face. I was about to say something, but before I could, I felt the atmosphere change. Change into something deadly. I look into his face. His eyes are narrow and... hostile, it sends chills down my spine. Fearful, I backed up. "Kris... Please don't look like that!" *'I wanted to approach him, but I'm too scared. Maybe I should let him be!'* I try to put a smile on my face. "I'll... I'll just let you be!" I turned and started walking, but I was pulled back. *'Lord, am I going to get killed?'*

CHAPTER EIGHT

Robin

His arm slips around my back, pulling me closer to him. I looked up at Kris, startled to find fire burning in his eyes. "Tell me why!" I try to look down, feeling a little anxious, but with his free hand he grips my chin, pulling my face closer to his. He stares me dead in my eyes! "Why is it that every time I see him, I see you and him together, you walk off with him, you do anything with him, I get so furious. I feel like I'm going to lose you. You have tried to leave once and I feel you'll try again. Robin, I'm not going to lie, but I'm scared! Scared of you hating me! Scared of the love you have for me will disappear!" A light smile crosses my face, I lean in gently kissing his lips. “My love for you has grown Kris! I won't run away from you because somehow, someway with you being a brute at times, your gentleness and loving childish self has finally reached my heart to where you mean so much to me!” He stares down at me, his hand sliding from my chin to the back of my head. His breathing becomes heavier as he pushes his lips onto mine, kissing me deeply. *'Oh how I love the feeling of his lips on mine!'* Kissing deeply, his tongue wrapped around mine, I closed my eyes enjoying the moment. His hands slowly travel to my hips and without warning he picks me up, breaking the kiss. "Eep!" Startled, I quickly wrapped my arms around his neck and my legs around his waist. "Lets head back! The wind is starting to pick up!" He turns and walks back to the house.

Once in his room, he lays me down, then covers me with his body. He kisses me hard, forcing me to lose my breath. "Kri... Kris!" I quietly moaned his name into the kiss, which seemed to make him more worked up. Next thing I know, his hands began to slide under my clothes, roaming my body. "Robin!" He moans my name. Slowly he undresses me, his touches on my skin burn and I can feel something ache inside me. I watch him undress, taking his time. Once his pants fell to the ground with his boxers I couldn't help my eyes from roaming over his hot body with his six pack hard abs down to his thick long throbbing cock. I lay there on the bed as his hands trail over my thighs, gripping them as he pries them apart. He adjusted himself between my legs, pressing his member up to my entrance before sliding deep inside me. He towers over me, staring me down. He places a hand over my breast squeezing then leans down, kissing me. I don't know how many times we have done it, but I know that my nails have scarred his back. With each thrust my moans would echo louder and louder in the room. "I love you Kris!" I screamed once we reached our climax. "I love you too Robin!" He kisses me before pulling out, then lays down next to me. Breathing heavily, he huffs, "Are you ok? We did it more than normal." I look at him a bit exhausted, giving him a small smile. "Yes!" I lightly peck him on his lips before falling into a deep sleep.

"Miss Robin! It's time to get up!" I open my eyes, revealing Kris's room. Yawning, I prop myself up. "What time is it?" I looked over at Melissa. "It's ten-thirty A.M. right now miss!" I move my hand to Kris... *'Where is he?'* "If you are looking for the Master, he has gone out." Melissa says, giving me a blouse, shorts and underwear that she got out of my closet. *'I guess he went out to work!'* I steadily stand to my feet, feeling a bit of pain. "Miss Robin, would you like to eat breakfast here?" I looked out the window. "How about we gather everyone and have a picnic, we'll have brunch!" She looks at me, "Yes miss!" She says, walking out with a smile.

Under the sun, by the pond me, my maid, and my ex butlers eat the meals that Melissa made, then after the meal some of us went swimming, some sat in the sun. For me I swung on the swing, shaded by the tree. "Sorry I'm late!" Derick walks out of the maze with his little sister, June, at hand. "I would have been here sooner, but I got caught up at work and when I got home June could not figure out what to wear." I stand from the swing then crouch down to June's level. She smiles, then her little arms wrap around my neck. At first I didn't quite comprehend the sudden hug, but brushing that off, I wrapped my arms around her. "Robin!" She steps back, staring up at me. "Will you marry Derick? If you do, we can be sisters!" She says as she rocks on her feet and grips at her dress. I stared at her, no words came out of my mouth. "June, what did I say about asking that!" Derick looks at me as I slowly stand to my feet. "I'm sorry Robin, she really likes you and would not stop talking about you." He gives me a light smile. I feel my heart skip a beat. *'His smile is so cute!'* "Uh.... ah... it's ok!" I stand, smiling. Looking at him, I notice his smile slowly fades and he is getting a bit closer. *'Wait.... what is he-'* His hand grabs my shoulder as the other tilts my head up a bit, forcing me to look into his brown eyes. "Robin!" I jump a bit as something tugs on my shirt. I looked down to see June. She doesn't speak, she just looks down and kicks her feet in the dirt. "What's wrong?" She raises her arm and points at the entrance of the maze. I slowly followed her arm, then noticed what made her so tense. It was Kris. My eyes widen, fear overcomes me as I stare at his expression, one that is deadly. *'Oh my god!'* "Ahh it's not-" I took a step forward but was pulled back. "Now you see! She doesn't want you, she chose me." Suddenly my head was pulled back and my lips were covered by another. *'What!'*

Sitting on the couch deep in my thoughts, I fail to notice the deep blue eyes staring down at me. After Derick kissed.... kissed me, my arm was pulled forcing me to stumble and land on Kris's chest. Kris wrapped an arm around my head and started to scream at Derick. *'I swear if I wasn't in Kris's arms he would have been swinging his fists right into Derick's face!'* When Kris has nothing else to say to Derick, he picks me up and heads back to the house. Fidgeting with the hem of my shirt, Kris reaches over covering my hands, entangling his fingers with mine, forcing them away from my shirt and snapping me out of my trance.

"Kris, before you say anything, I just want to say what happened back there was nothing-" "That was nothing! Heh!" He leans in closer to me forcing me to sink into the couch. "He kissed you and you did nothing to stop it! I thought you told me I could trust you? Why was he so close to you to begin with?" "You can trust me, it just all happened so fast and-" I shouted back before he cut me off. "Then prove it to me! Prove to me that I can trust you! Meet me in my room tonight, and be ready for punishment." With that said, he stands from his seat, his hand pulled away from mine leaving a longing feeling deep in my heart. He storms off before I can say another word. *'None of this was supposed to happen, I just wanted a nice picnic with everyone!'* I covered my face as tears slowly streamed down my cheeks.

I crouch in the corner of my room waiting for night to fall. Waves of sadness and confusion hit me, one can now see tear stains on my cheeks, eyes puffy and red. I keep hearing shuffling of feet on the other side of my room door, the sound of the door-knob, knocking, along with Rex's and Melissa calling my name. I don't move from my spot, not an inch. I just kept my arms around my legs, pulled into my chest and my face buried into my knees.

The lit room from the sun slowly becomes involved into darkness only leaving a ray of light from the moon. Slowly, I stand from my spot, trudge my way to the door unlocking it then head down the hall to Kris's room. My hair was a mess, makeup smeared, tears still going down my face... I looked like a mess. Suddenly my arm jerked back, turning me around. "Derick? What?" My words sound shaky. Derick looks into my eyes that have become dull. He pulls me in close and picks me up. "Nooo I have to see Kris!" I fight against him but I'm too weak. He easily slings me over his shoulder and walks outside with me screaming. “Oh my god Derick, haven't you done enough damage! My eyes closed as I banged on his back, screeching for help. "Kris! Rex! Anybody!" When I do, I hear voices and hurried footsteps getting closer. "Kris, help me!" I cry out right before I'm thrown into a limo followed by Derick. Next thing I know the car speeds off and I see everyone running after the car. I quickly slid further away from him. "Where are you taking me?" "To France!" My eyes widened. "What? No! I can't!" I quickly reach for the handle and pull it, only to find it's locked on the inside. I started to slam the windows and doors, yelling and sobbing. "Robin, please calm down!" He wraps his arms around me and holds me close. "No! I will not 'calm down'! Take me back." I demanded and pushed on his chest. "I'm sorry, but I can't do that. I love you!" Next thing I know, my mouth is covered by a cloth and a few minutes later I black out.

"Mmm!" I move around, my eyes opening and closing until everything stops spinning. I sit up, placing a hand on my head as a pulsing headache grows. I look around, half groggy. I am in a bed that is silky white and the only other thing in the light blue room is a big white door and a small bedside table with a glass of water and a pill bottle that I quickly grab and swallow before the pain gets any worse. *‘Ugg... I hate having headaches! I'm unable to focus.’*

After a bit of sitting there, the pain becoming only slightly painful, I steadily crawl across the bed and reach for the knob, extending my arm out to it as far as my arm could go. I lean a bit further over the end of the bed. "Almost!" Leaning more, my hand slides closer to the edge, and when I do, the tip of my finger touches the knob. I smile and reach further, but the arm I'm leaning on slips and I fall to the floor. I quickly stand to my feet, brushing off my clothes. I look forward and stand still for a bit. *'... I feel like I'm swaying a bit.'* I looked around for a window, but there wasn't one. I bit my bottom lip and swung open the door to a long hallway. Cautiously I take a step forward, then another, and without a split second I sprint down, swaying left and right. After a bit I reach another door and push it open with my body leading into it. It swings open when a gust of wind hits the door causing me to lose my balance and fall onto the deck, my head hitting the ground. “Ahh didn't this happen once before?” Standing with my hand on my head, leaning over my legs, I pause in my tracks hearing the sound of waves along with a whiff of salt water hitting my nose. I sit up straight and with bewilderment I head to the railing to only see the open sea. *'Where the hell am I?'*

While thinking of what to do, arms wrap around my waist. "You're awake!" I look up to see Derick. "Where are you taking me?" I turn my head back to the sea. "To France!" He hugs me a bit tighter. "Why not by plane?" I slowly shove him off and walk away. "Mmm I thought it would be nicer like this, plus one of your wishes was to go on a cruise right?" He grabs my hand and walks with me. "I.... I guess, but this isn't what I meant. I was hoping to be with family and friends more." I pulled my hand away before running off. I look around, not knowing what to do or where to go. Tears swell up in my eyes as my legs finally give up on me, making me fall to my knees. I hung my head. "Robin?" I look up to see June, who smiles as bright as always. I rubbed my eyes. "Oh... hey girly!" I hold my arms out to her and she embarrasses me. "Why are you crying?" She asked, hugging me tighter. "I'm not crying, I'm ok." I lightly pull her back and look into her brown eyes and brush my fingers through her red hair. "How about we have some fun?" Her eyes widened. "Yes please!" She grabs my hand and starts pulling me.

"Where are we going?" I ask as I'm being pulled along by this small, cheerful child. "I need my swimsuit!" She says. "But I don't have one!" I reply! She stops and looks up at me smiling brightly. "That's ok, big brother made sure to make a personal changing room just for us." She lets out a cute laugh before turning and walking faster towards that changing room. It didn't take too long to get there and once we did June already started throwing clothes off. "Ah! What about this?" She pulls out a one piece bathing suit that's covered with flower printing. "That's really cute!" I say, bending down to her level. "Hehe!" She twirls before running into the dressing room and after it's on she runs out. "Ok! Your turn!" She starts to dig in the adult section of the room. "Oh! This would look amazing on you!" She pulls out a two piece bikini. It was black with a pink rim Triangle Halter Neck Drawstring Tie Back Tie Side High Cut Two Piece Bikini. I blush trying to think of what to say. "Umm... What about something like yours?" She shakes her head. "No, it has to be this one!" I grabbed it and slipped into the dressing room. I held up the bikini, blushing brightly.

'Why did she have to choose this one? It's showing so much skin!' I slipped it on and walked out, but before I could do anything else I was once again dragged out the door and headed to her next location.

Once at the pool, June throws down her towel on a chair and dives in. Smiling, I sit down on the edge, feet hanging in the water. The water felt cold at first but became warm after a while. Bit by bit I inched into the water, but didn't get far because I was suddenly shoved in. *'What on earth!'* My eyes are open wide and I can't breathe, I swim to the top coughing. I looked up to see Derick crouching where I was sitting, laughing. I tear up a bit and swim back to the edge, climbing out. He quickly stands up, grabbing my arm and pulling me back to the ground. "Robin! I'm sorry I wasn't trying to make you mad!" I jerked my arm back away from him glaring with hatred. "Well you should have thought about that before you kidnapped me." Then I stormed back to the room that I woke up in. I sit on the bed thinking of what to do. I rubbed my eyes sniffling. *'I wonder how Kris and my parents are doing? Oh how I miss them so much!'* Slowly I start to drift off from the soothing motion of the cruise. My eyes closed as I heard the creaking of the room door. "Robin?" I hear June's voice echo in the room and the bed starts to dip as she crawls over to me, snuggling up to me and kissing my cheek. "Night night!" She lays down next to me and she drifts off to sleep.

Uncomfortable, my eyes flutter open in the dark room. I sit up and rub my eyes and carefully slide off the bed, heading to the door. I opened the door slightly letting light seeping through the room and on my bed I saw two figures, one small child and the other a tall man. I lean against the door looking at them for a bit before walking out, shutting the door behind me. I walk down the hall and out to the deck. I looked over the rail and stretched a bit as the smell of salt filled my nose. I walk down the cruise in search of the dining room, rocking with the waves. After a good while of searching I found it, I sat down as eggs, bacon, toast, and milk was placed in front of me. I look at the Butler in the corner of my eyes. A tall old man, with a gray mustache and little stubs on his chin, his head half way bald. "Thank you!" I say lightly as he walks away. I look at the food as I feel my stomach turn. *'Ugg I'm going to throw up if I eat this, I don't feel too well!'* I stand up, not touching the food, and walk away back out on the deck and circle the cruise looking for a way off or at least a way to contact someone. Tired from walking for hours, I lean against a wall and slide down it, sighing. "Looks like I'm just going to have to wait this out till we reach France.... But how long will it take till we get there." I wine loudly, falling over on the cold wooden floor.

CHAPTER NINE

Robin

Rolling over on to my side as a shiver creeps up my spine, I pull closer to me, gripping it tightly. I sit still for a bit before laying back down on my back and feeling around. *'I'm in bed... But how?'* I open my eyes and sit up quickly looking around, only to find myself back in the empty, pitch black room. Sighing, I pull my legs up to my chest and wrap my arms around them, burying my face in my legs. "I'm still here!" I say, my voice muffled.

Sitting there I hear stomping outside the door then it swings open and slams into the wall, causing me to jump, jerking my head up to see a tall figure stepping into "my room". At the end of the bed, Derick looks down at me smiling. I feel my eyes twitch. 'He's starting to piss me off!' "What do you want?" I huffed. His smile grows, then out of nowhere he tackles me on the bed and starts to tickle me. Laughing and squirming, I yell out to him, tearing up a bit. "Noooo stop!" He laughs, then he finally stops after a bit. I look up at him breathing kind of hard. "What's wrong with you?" He nuzzles his face into mine. "Just trying to lighten the mood and to get you to change your frown upside down." Pouting, I roll over to avoid him. "Well whose fault is that!" "Ah come on, I said I'm sorry, I don't want you mad at me! I did this so we could be together." I quickly sat up. "But I don't love you, I love Kris and was happy until you came around! You've ruined everything!" I laid back down and covered myself up in the sheets. "Do you remember as a kid before I left we made flower promise rings, that day we made a vow that we would love each other till the end. Together forever till death shall we part!" I felt my eye twitch again and sat back up, the sheets pushed off of me. I looked straight into his eyes, mine narrowing at him. My hand swings, my palm hitting his face. "We were kids making a silly promise, you left and I felt alone again. Over time I've never seen you since, and as time passed that promise was forgotten and I fell out of love with you." I notice his eye color go darker as he holds his cheek looking at me with a bit of shock. "But the love you have for him isn't even love, it's only you thanking your in love. He's gotten inside your head and manipulated you, he's using you. I bet he's sleeping with every girl on the block, having you in his back pocket! You're his pet waiting on their master locked up in that house." My eyes tear up, tears streaming down my cheeks. "Get out!" His expression softens. "Robin, I'm sor-" "Get out of this room, now!" I shouted louder, pointing at the door. He looks at me speechless, slowly sliding off the bed and heading out the door, slamming it behind him.

It's already been 2 and a half weeks since we left the US and during that time I've done my best to avoid and ignore Derick. I spent most of my time in my room watching movies or reading a book or with June playing and having fun, all the things you would do with a kid. "Would you like more tea Miss Lee?" She says sweetly, lifting the tea pitcher to my cup. "I would love some lady Abernathy!" She pours the tea into my cup. "Thank you very much. Would you like some finger sandwiches with your tea?" I held up the plate. "I'd be delighted!" She reaches her little arms across her little kids table, but right before her fingers could touch the food, the door swings open, startling us, causing June to almost fall out of her chair. "Where here!" Derick says, shouting. My eyes open wide and I quickly head to the door, running down the hall and to the deck. Leaning against the rail I look out to see the scenery. My heart starts to race, my eyes sparkle as I'm amazed by the view. *'Oh my god, France looks so beautiful! I can't believe I've finally come!'* Forgetting my worries, I lean further over the rail, a bit too excited. "Woah there, you're going to fall over bored!" Arms wrapped around my waist, pulling me in. Derick holds me close and from this my cheeks become flushed. "Wait! No!" I shove him off and back away. "Robin I truly love you and you know you feel the same, so why don't you just stop pushing me away and denying your feelings for me."

My cheeks start to burn with rage, but in the corner of my eye June is watching us. Slowly I close my eyes and breathe in a deep breath. "I told you before and that what you're saying with me having love for you still, it's gone for good, so let it be and let me go. I'll admit I'm really happy to see France for once, but the way I got here was a disaster. I mean why couldn't we have brought others along, why can't you accept me being with Kris, why does it-" My lips were covered before I could finish. Looking at him I noticed him closing the gap. "No more please! Don't talk about him anymore either! I just.... I just thought maybe there could still be love from when we were kids. Maybe you'd forgive me for leaving so long ago." I notice him slowly dropping to one knee. "You've always meant so much to me and I could never forget about you, you seriously mean the world to me and I would do anything for you." I watched him pull something out of his jacket and I could already feel my heart drop. *'Oh no, déjà vu!'* "Yes, maybe I have gone too far being pushy and persistent, but there's no limits to how much I love you and what I would do for you!" He holds out a little box and opens it. Inside is a diamond flower ring exactly like the real flower promise ring from when we were kids, but silver. Tears pierce my eyes, my hands covering my mouth. "I..." He looks down already knowing my answer. He stands closing the box and grabs my hand. "Please take this and think about it." Once in my hands he walks off, his head hanging low. Once out of sight I open the box again and trace it with the tip of my finger against the flower petals. *'What do I do?'*

I walk down the deck looking around, a huge garden in my view and in the far distance is a huge mansion. "Oh my gosh, is that really Robin?" I hear a woman say in excitement. Once on the ground she hurried to me grabbing my hands then pulling me in a hug. "Oh my goodness! I haven't seen you since you were a little girl. Look how you've grown into such a beautiful woman." I stand there frozen, searching through my memories. "Oh my lord Mrs. Abernathy, it's been so long!" I smile, my arms wrapped around her, hugging her back. "Please love, call me Mary! When Derick called and told me you were coming to visit I was just so thrilled. How have your parents been? Are they doing well?" Mary pulls back and grabs my hand in hers. "Come, we must go and discuss everything over a cup of tea!" She starts to pull me into her car, the driver holding the door open. I turned my head to look back at Derick to see what he would say, only to find a big grin on his face. Before I know it, I'm sitting in between both Derick and his mother. *'.... I feel a tad smothered with them all up on me like this.'* Mary holds tightly on my arm talking away about how their life has been since they moved to France, as Derick slides his hand into mine squeezing a bit. "Mommy, why can't I sit with Robin?" I look up to see little June sitting across from us, her hands folded on her lap, pouting as she stares at how close her mother and brother are to me. "Oh I'm sorry dear, I just got so excited after not getting to see her for such a long time." Mary leans her head towards me. "I've tried to convince your mother and father to come visit us, but they would always have an excuse or they would come without you." My eyes widened. *'Mother and father still kept in contact with the Abernathy's? They told me they've lost all contact since Mary and them moved to France!'* I looked up at Derick. "Oh you'll just love your room, I fixed it up myself." Mary says as we pull up to the back doors of the mansion.

Derick steps out once the car door is open, and he reaches out an arm towards me. I grab onto his arm and slowly step out.

"Thank you!" I say as I pull away from him. He goes to lend his arm to his mother and sister as my head starts to tilt up at how large their home is. "Isn't it just wonderful? I know you'll just love it here!" Mary begins to ramble as she walks up the steps to her home. June slides her hand into mine. "Want to see my room?" She says with a big smile on her face. "Hehe of course I'd love to see your room, just hold on to my hand so I don't get lost ok?" June nods before I follow her up the steps and inside the building, leaving Derick behind. June quickly drags me up the stairs and down the hall to a big door. She reaches up with her hand and twists the door knob. June pushed hard on the door, "What would you like to play first? Dolls, a tea party, family?" She let go of my hand and ran around the room picking up one thing after another. A smile grows on my face watching her. "Hey June, would you like to play restaurant?" June looks up at me. "Is that like a tea party?" She asked me, tilting her head a bit. I lean down to her level. "Hehe yes, but instead of us both at the table one of us will have to be the cook and waiter! Would you like to make a menu with me?" I point over to the arts and crafts station. She nods furiously and runs over to it, pulling out the paper and markers.

Once we finish the menu I will scan it over a bit. "This looks pretty good!" She smiles brightly, then suddenly shoots out of her chair, snatching the paper from my hands. "Oh my gosh!" She squeaks. "Make some more of these, I'll be right back!" She hurried out the door and out of my view. I look down at the papers laughing a bit. *'She's such a cutie!'* "Would you like some help?" I turn my head to look back at the door to see Derick walking over to the little table and sits across from me. He picks up the marker and pulls out some paper. "So what did the menu look like?" I stare at him for a minute, spacing out. ".... Oh um, chicken tenders, hamburgers, macaroni and cheese, you know the restaurant stuff! Nothing fancy!" I shrug, writing down everything once again on the paper. "Oh?" He leans towards me a bit. When he does, I quickly pull back. He then reached over, pulling my menu closer to him, it down onto his own sheet. "How many do you need?" He asked me as he's working on the drinks. "Just two more!" I say to him, not giving him a second glance. He noticed and I began to hear him tapping on the table. *'Mmm so this and this and.....'* I'm working on another menu when I hear a chair fall and I'm suddenly grabbed by the wrist. He pulls me to my feet then picks me up, wrapping my legs around his waist and pushing my back to the wall. "How long do you plan on avoiding me!" I looked down but he grabbed my chin and smashed his lips onto mine. *'It hurts!'* Tears slide down my cheeks as a wave of pain rushes through. Our lips part, and his eyes trail down to my painfully swollen lips. His hold on me tightens as he turns then carries me out of the room and down the hall.

Keeping my head down he opens the door to a room and sets me on the bed. "I..." He stops there, biting his bottom lip, his hands ball up into a fist as if fighting back something then walks out as fast as he came. *'What the hell am I going to do, I'm in another country and no way home.'* Wiping my lip with the back of my hand, I fall over on the bed. I lie there, my mind still trying to process what just happened and what I should do to get out of this mess. A light knock comes from the door before it slowly creeks open. “Darling, are you awake?” Mary says, walking up to the bed and sitting down on the edge. “Would you like to come down for dinner, dear? June says yall made something special for tonight!” Taking a deep breath and putting a smile on my face, I sit up. “Sorry I needed to rest for a bit! That cruise trip kind of wore me out. I feel better now.” I stand from the bed and she wraps her arm around mine, we slowly head to the dining room. In the room Mr. Abernathy and Darik are already sitting down. Mary sits me down next to Darik. Looking around I ask “Where is June?” “Sorry sorry I'm coming!” She walks around the room handing everyone at the table the menu we made right before sitting on the other side of me. “Ohhh this looks like a really good selection! I don't know what to choose.” I hear Mary say in delight. A butler comes and takes our order then heads into the kitchen as another butler comes out pouring our drinks. We sat in silence for a good while until our food arrived. “So Robin, I thought you'd like to decide when y'all's wedding would be!” My head shoots up at Mary, then to Darik, who almost chokes on his food. *‘What the heck, did he tell her something?’* “Ah mother we should probably talk about this another time-“ “Oh nonsense!” Mary cuts Darik off. “I heard you already proposed. We should start planning now. Ohh honey, we should have an engagement party!” She turns to her husband. I grip the silverware, feeling my stomach turn. Slowly standing, “Please excuse me, I'm not feeling well!” I say before sprinting off to my room.

CHAPTER TEN

Kris

It's been weeks since I've seen her or heard from her. *'I miss her! Uggg what do I do!'* I rubbed my temples, racking my brain for a solution. I would have left right away when she went missing, but due to me owning a company and Abernathy's are definitely not one to be trifled with, they are just as powerful. I stood from my chair, "Rex!" I called out. He opens the door and lightly bows his head. “I need an idea or reason.. An excuse for all I care to head to France, without starting conflict or raising suspicion if possible!” Rex placed his hand on his chin, thanking. "Well sir, there is one thing I can manage for you, a business opportunity, one that will make Abernathy's hard to refuse." He stands tall looking straight at me as a grin grows on my face. "And what will this “business opportunity” be, might I ask?" "Well sir, with both jewelry companies competing all the time and you just finding a new source of land with many diamonds at your disposal, what about a collaboration with one another or at least a deal to supply them the diamonds?" Crossing my arms I tilt my head to the side, considering his idea. "That sounds like a pretty good plan!" I turn and begin grabbing my paperwork off my desk. "Rex, prepare my private jet and reach out to the Abernathys giving them the proposal, let them decide which to choose from! In the meantime I need to make a few calls and get a few things, we are heading to France!"

On my jet, I'm talking to Rex over the phone, listening as best I can to the details over the plan and on all that he has accomplished for it to go smoothly, though I become out of it as my head begins throbbing, leaving me unable to fully focus. "Rex, can you fax me all this information so I can go over it later?" "Yes, of course sir! I wish you well on your flight!" He responded before hanging up. My head falls into my hands as images of Robin run through my head. *'Oh Robin, I miss you so much!'* Slowly everything begins to go black as I drift into darkness.

Loud screeching wakes me from my slumber! "Sir, you need to get off this jet now!" The air pilot shoves a parachute into my arms as he drags me to my feet while I'm still in a daze. Before I could grab any of the paperwork he had already shoved me to the door, swinging it open. "Excuse me sir!" He says as I feel his hands on my back and the next thing I know I'm falling. "Sir, when you get a bit closer pull the string!" I could barely hear him due to the distance between us. I watched as the ocean below got closer and closer, I pulled the string.... Nothing.... I pull the other sting.... Nothing. *'This son of a bitch, this was a set up!'* Falling faster and faster I watched as the water got closer and before plummeting into the sea I drew in my last breath.

"Oh my goodness! Sir, are you ok?" I feel someone pull on my arms and then hands engulf my face. My eyes slowly flutter open to see a woman with long wavy black hair and emerald green eyes. Coughing up water, I try my best to respond, "Just feeling a bit sore!" She turns her head and calls some people over as she attempts to sit me up. Two other men grab my arms lifting me onto my feet. *'What the hell's going on? Where am I?'* I stare at these people in confusion as they drag me into a large home and lay me onto a couch. "Uggg, who are you?" I asked in pain. "My name is Darcey Sable, and may I ask who you are?" She asked me as she placed a wrap on my head. I sat there, thanking, eyes squinting. "I... I don't know!" I admit. I see her eyes soften and for some reason I just want to hug her, telling her that everything will be ok. "Mhmm well sir I hope you don't mind, but until your memory comes back would you mind me calling you Henry?" I nodded my head. "That's fine!"

All day Darcy hasn't left my side, she's been taking really good care of me and has even got her servants to set a room up for me. *'She's so cute and sweet, but why do I feel like something isn't right?'* I watch her go around, sit next to me and turn on the tv. She flips through the channels until she hits a vampire show. We sat there watching the show for a good while. By the time it was over it was already dark and Darcy had already passed out on the couch. I stand up off the couch and walk over to her with a cover in my hands and gently tuck her in. I then head upstairs to my room and shut the door behind me. My hand slides up to my head, brushing my fingers through my brown hair. *'Why does my chest hurt so much?'* Huffing, I trudge over to the bed then fall on it, pulling the covers over me and trying to get some rest but just to find myself staring into the darkness, this emptiness inside me growing from the spot next to me felt so empty.

Light knocking comes from the door, I turn my head looking at it as it creaks open. *'Seems I stayed up all night!'* I'm sitting up in bed as Darcy's head pops out from the doorway. "Good morning! I just wanted to let you know breakfast is ready and to see if you wanted to come down or if you'd rather have breakfast in bed?" I go to stand off the bed only to feel a sharp throbbing pain shoot through my head. I grab my temple, leaning on the bed hunched over, the pain causing me to grind my teeth together as my jaw clenches. "I'll come down!" I respond as I shake my head hoping to ignore the aching pain. Slowly I got up from the bed, feet planted to the ground then out the door, but I wasn't able to make it far due to the images of a girl flashing before my eyes which caused the pain to increase. I lean against the wall as Darcy grabs onto me trying to help me. "Oh my god, are you ok?" She screeched. I catch my footing, pulling my arm away from her unconsciously. I stare at her a bit in shock from my actions, her face showing the same expression. "I'm good, let's go!" I look away from her, becoming annoyed with myself and my behavior.

"So I was thanking... There is a party tonight at the Abernathy mansion! Would you be willing to go with me?" Her hands clasped together, her head tilted and a smile glowed on her face. My lips thin due to the thought of crowds bothering me though I'm relieved with the change of topic. Slowly I nod and she jumps in joy grabbing my hands and pecking my lips. She blushes and pulls back. “I'm so sorry... It's just that...I know it hasn't been long since we met, but I think you're quite handsome and I really like you so...” She trails off, her lips quivering. Staring down at her frail look I couldn't help but feel indebted to her so without thanking I lightly grabbed her hand that toyed with her dress. “How about we get engaged?” I saw her eyes light up as she squeezed my hand. “Oh my god! Really?” Without me responding, she jumps on me, kissing me harder than before, then turns around exhilarated. "Ohhh I need to get you a suit! I'll get one that matches my dress!" She swiftly takes out her phone and begins typing on it as she leaps down the stairs. When she's gone I let out a sigh of relief and look out the window. *'Why do I feel like something isn't right!'* I look around this dull hallway, nothing filling familiar causes me more anxiety. *'Who the hell am I?'*

Laying on the couch, staring up at the ceiling, I hear a few doors slam and a woman that is starting to become quite a grating voice, echoes in the house. "Darling I'm home, I got you so much!" My head falls to the side to look out the window. *'Have I really laid here all day?'* With a heavy sigh I slowly lifted myself off the couch and onto my feet, fixing my shirt. "I'm so excited, will you try this on?" Darcy storms in as I bring my arms down and pushes a suit into my chest. "You can change here, I'll be in the bathroom!" That's all she said before this small woman scurried into the bathroom.

Stepping out of the car, I stand tall, stretching my back as the small black-haired woman stumbles out of it. I quickly wrapped my arm around her waist, pulling her closer to me, keeping her footing stable. With her now on my side gripping my shirt, we follow the red carpet to the inside of the large mansion. Music and chatter echo in the room as we walk further into the crowd. *'I've barely been in here and I'm already getting a headache!'* I scan around the room, my eyes stopping on a young blonde woman. '*She looks so familiar!'* I then noticed a man move next to her, sliding his arm around her, pulling her in. My fists clenched as I noticed her head move down looking at the floor, anger rising inside me and without noticing, I had taken a few quick steps forward, causing Darcy to be dragged. "Henry?" I look down at Darcy as she steadies herself before sliding her hands into mine. "Let's dance!" She pulls me into the crowd with a wide smile on her face.

We slowly swayed with the crowd, it wouldn't have been that bad if Darcy would stop talking about so many things, for one I can't keep up and it really doesn't make a lot of sense to me. 'She's *been rambling on so much about her plans for her future engagement party, wedding, family and children. She seems to be wanting a wedding grander than the one we are at... Plus some more things!'* I scoff at the thought of it. '*This man seems way more powerful, even though her family's in the upper class, he seems to have more power judging by the way his home and this party is. His home minus will be a castle!'* Lost in my thoughts, my eyes gaze back at the blonde girl as she holds herself, keeping her distance from the crowd. I want to go over and hug her... kiss her... I want her...

"Hey Henry!" Darcy waves a hand in my face. "Did you hear me? What do you think of my wedding idea for us... or is a wedding in the next four months for us too soon?" Taking a deep breath I close my eyes then look at Darcy. She bites her bottom lip looking down. "Maybe we can talk more about this another day! I'm feeling a bit parched, would you like a drink?" Before she could answer, my arms slipped away from her and I strode off. "Ah... ok, I'll wait here and chat with some of my friends then while you get it!"

I reach the table and pick up two glasses then turn back to the crowd. I scanned the area a bit before letting out a sigh. *'I guess I'm a bit too far away to see her from here!'* Ploddingly I started to walk back into the crowd, getting closer I saw Darcy twirling with her friends, her smile growing. *'What the hell am I thanking, looking at another woman when I'm engaged. She saved my life and has been beside me all this time. I owe her and here I am being a disgrace to my savior... my future wife!'* I speed up my steps and am right back to her. "Hey babe drink something, you've been dancing for a while!" She turns around from her friends. "Hehe! What took you so long?" She takes a cup from my hand and slowly sips it. "Sorry I was a bit lost in my thoughts!" I lean down before lightly kissing her cheek. I hear her friends squeal as Darcy's cheeks turn red. "Hurry and drink up then let's get back to dancing a bit longer!" I give her a light smile before finishing my cup and handing it to a waiter then walking further into the crowd. She quickly chugs her drink, shoves it at the waiter and hurries after me, jumping into my open arms.

CHAPTER ELEVEN

Robin

I slid my hand over my arm, gripping it as Derick's arm wrapped around my waist, pulling me closer to him. I keep my head low, biting my bottom lip. '*I hate this! I've tried to stop this, but again I've been put in a position where no one will listen to me.*' Slowly I look up from the ground spotting a very familiar face.... Kris... my Kris. A smile grew on my face before I sprinted forward into the crowd "Robin!" I hear Derick yell as he reaches for me. I move away and disappear onto the dance floor. I squeezed around people, pushing them aside as my heart rate sped up. '*Oh my god! I've never been so happy like this! I can't believe he came for me, I was starting to lose hope since it's been so long!*'

Seeing him right within my reach, I lunged forward a bit to excite, causing me to stumble over a couple. '*Oh no!*' I close my eyes, tearing up as I wait for the hard ground... Only to have hands grip my arms pulling me close to a solid chest... one I've missed so dearly. I look up to see my beloved Kris. I couldn't help but smile and pull him in for a kiss. *'I've missed this warmth... but something seems off!'* I noticed how he didn't hold me close... he didn't even kiss me back. All that happened was him lightly pushing my shoulders back and before a word was said I was turned around then a palm was smashed into my face.... It all happened so fast!

"How dare you kiss my fiancé!" A dark-haired woman screeches into my face before grabbing onto Kris's arm. I stand there stunned holding my cheek. *'Her... Her fiancé? So he's over me? He wasn't here for me, he came to tell me he had moved on!'* Tears swell up in my eyes. "What the hell is going on here?" A hand covers my eyes as a chest is pushed up against my back. "Who the fuck do you think you are to raise your hand at her!" I hear a voice roar in anger above my head. "Oh... D... Derick! I'm so sorry to disturb your party, I'm just teaching this wretched bit..." "Don't you dare cuss at my love! Who do you thank this party is for?" I can't see what's going on but Derick's grip on me tightens as I hear the lady stumble on her words. "And you Kris, who invited you here?" I slowly pulled Derick's hand down from my face, my eyes slowly looking up at Kris wanting an explanation only to find him giving us a confused look. "Heh, you know, never mind! I knew you weren't really in love with Robin!" Derick then picks me up, walks off and out of the party as Kris slowly looks down at the ground. I'm assuming lost in thought as the black haired girl moves closer to him, placing her hand on his back.

I'm sitting on the edge of my bed going through the whole incident through my head as a tall man is pacing around my floor. "I'm so sorry you had to find out the truth like this love!" He comes to a stop and kneels down in front of me, grabbing my hands. "He should not have come here today and I promise you, you will never have to see him again!" He says looking up at me... but I can't look at him. *'This whole thing just doesn't feel right, but I can't put my finger on it!'* "Robin, I will not force you to marry me, but you can not leave me, not after what happened today." Derick stands, letting go of my hands. "I refuse to let you be around a scoundrel like that, you deserve better... No, you deserve the best this world has to offer." He walks to the door, opening it. "Get some rest, I'll have a maid come up and check on you!" He shuts the door behind him leaving me to my thoughts.

Restless, I stand from the bed and trudge to the window, looking through it. Steadily my hand reaches for the handle, pulling the window open. I pushed it further, feeling the breeze hit my face. Leaning further out, I close my eyes, breathing in a deep breath. "Malady?" A woman grabbed my arm. Looking at her a bit surprised, I noticed worry and concern grow on her face. "Ah... sorry! I was feeling a bit stuffy here." Pushing my hair behind my ear I close the window before heading my way back to the bed. "What can I do for you?" Sitting back down I cross my arms looking down at the floor. "I was just coming to see if the lady needed anything?" She stands in front of me with her hands untwined. *'What I want is to go home!'* Slowly my hands slide over my stomach. '*Ugg, lately I've been feeling nauseous!*' "Would you like me to bring you something to eat? For an appetizer we have escargots and for the main course they are serving sole meunière-" Quickly I stand from the bed rushing to the bathroom, my shoulder colliding into hers in the process. "Malady, is everything-" I slammed the door behind me before she could finish her sentence and hover over the toilet, my insides draining from my stomach.

"Robin what's going on!" Derick hurries into the bathroom and is at my side with a hand on my back as I gag a few more times. '*That dame maid had to screech into the hall!*' "I hurried as fast as I could when Miss Moulin shouted for help!" He goes to hold my hair but I raise a hand to stop him. I flush the toilet then stand rubbing my mouth with the back of my hand and walking off to the sink, avoiding all contact with him, and I reply, "I'm fine!" I wash my hands then head out to the door of the room. "Now I would like to rest so can you both please leave!" They look at one another before heading out. Derick walks out first with Miss Moulin following. I reach out grabbing her arm and say in a light voice, "Though if you don't mind, can you bring me something for nausea and something light to eat please? Maybe soup?" She nods. "Yes, malady!" Once alone again I let out a sigh of relief and looked down at my stomach. '*I know I've been feeling nauseous lately but it seems to be getting worse... And now that I think about it I am late for my period!*'

"Holy shit!" I shout out then hurry to the door, throwing it open. I ran down the hall and down the stairs to the front door.

"Robin! What's wrong?" I hear Derick ask. Quickly I rushed out the door shouting, "Where's the closet store!" Derick runs after me grabbing my arm. "If you need to go to the store you could have just asked a maid!" "No! I need something from the store now... I'll either run there or you take me, either way I'm in a hurry!" I jerked my arm away from him. He looks down at me. "Edmé! Bring me the car!" He shouts.

We headed out in the car, I sat across Derick at a loss for words on what was going on with my body. "So if you don't mind me asking," he says, breaking the silence. "What was so urgent you needed to go to the store for?" Thinning my lips, staring down at my feet, I lightly spoke, "The reason for me needing to go to the store is none of your business... Even so, until it is confirmed then I will tell you!" He stays silent, nodding his head. '*Though if I'm really pregnant what am I going to do? Kris doesn't love me anymore... or whatever the hell's going on with him. I'm in France away from my loved ones. I'm alone!*' "Derick, I want you to promise me one thing!" I say, grabbing his arm and squeezing. "What is it, Robin? I'll do anything for you!" My eyes narrow from his words. "It's not something you need to do but a promise I need you to keep, whatever happens you will never force me to do anything I don't want to do which includes the wedding!" He grabs my hands back, his thumb tracing across my skin, he opens his mouth to speak, but before he could get a word out I said, "With the wedding issue, at least until I'm ready... Please!" He pauses for a moment, a smile growing on his face. He pulls my hands to his lips and lightly kisses them. "It's a promise!"

It took a while to get to the store, then back to Derick's home, and my anxiety spiked as I gripped the pregnancy test in my chest as I walked to the bathroom, Derick hot on my tail. '*It was a bit embarrassing at the store because he was so persistent on going in with me, but I managed to get it without him knowing... but if I was pregnant how would he react! Being stuck here, I have nowhere to go if I get kicked out! I have no money nor a phone to reach anyone!*' "Please wait here!" I asked before heading into my room and shutting the door on Derick, then quickly rushed into the bathroom, locking it behind me. I stare at the test in my hand shaking with what I believe is fear... or could this feeling be something else? Anticipation? Joy? '*My emotions are all over the place!*'

CHAPTER TWELVE

Kris

The day happened in a blur. I looked at the girl that was pulled away and out of my view. I hear Darcey huff in anger as she squeezes my arms into her chest. "Let's get out of here!" I was pulled to the entrance breathing in the fresh air. *'What is this strange feeling?'* A wave of anger flows through me as my mind keeps replaying that man pulling that woman from me. I want to rush back in there and pick her up. I want to hold her close to me, kissing her deeply.... Show everyone in that room who she belongs to. "Dear?" I feel a tug on my shirt, my gaze lowers to look into the women's saddened eyes. "When she kissed you did you fall for her?" A tear strays from her eyes. *'Shit! I'm doing it again!'* I brush my thumb across her cheek. "Of course not Darcey, you're the only one for me." Lowering myself down to her level, I lean in to kiss her but stop mid way. She stares at me blankly, then leans in to meet me halfway, but without thanking, I pull away, my eyes narrowing. "I'm sorry, I'm really tired. Let's head back!"

At the house I head to my room and strip off my clothes before sliding into a cold shower. My finger brushed through my hair, my mind fogged with thoughts... Thoughts I shouldn't be having. "Tss!" I hold my head as pain shoots through. Leaning against the wall I hear a woman whisper in my ear "Wakey wakey darling" my head rises, spotting her... that woman from the party. Then when I blink the images stop. I hit the wall breathing heavily. *'Why... Why are you on my mind and what are these memories!'*

Laying on the bed I read the newspaper trying to get my mind off of things. "Honey?" The door opens and Darcey walks in, shuts the door and jumps on my bed. "What can I do for you Darcey?" Her lips thin, her eyebrows narrow, and she slides closer to me, her hand sliding over my shirt. "Why can't you sound sweeter to me?" I laid the paper to the side and looked at her. "What do you me-" she suddenly grips my shirt, her leg swings over me to wear she's straddling my lap, her lips pushed up against mine. I stared, stunned! I feel her hands trace down to my jeans and her fingers try to unbutton them. I quickly grabbed her by the shoulders, pulling her back. "What on earth are you doing!" I see her fingers curl up in a ball. "What do you mean? Am I that unpleasant, that you won't kiss me back, let alone make love to me? You said you love me and you said you'd marry me, but I've gotten nothing from you other than your empty words!" She tries to lean back in as she lightly places her hands on my cheeks. I cover her lips with the palm of my hand. "Darcey, I'm sorry! I do care for you, but it's just not that way and I'd hate to put you in a loveless relationship especially when I have no arousal to you!" I pick her up and move her to the side before standing off the bed. "I do appreciate everything you have done for me, but I don't think I can let this go on any further. If there is another way to repay you for your kindness and so much more please let me know. You can sleep here, I'll ask the maids for another room!" Quickly I storm off, heading down the dark empty hallway.

Sitting on the edge of the bed I stare into space. *'I can't sleep!'* I stand and stride to the door then walk down the halls, next thing I know I'm standing outside. "Sir, is everything alright?" Darcy's butler walks up to me. I glance over, "I'm fine... I'm going for a walk!" I headed off onto the sidewalk leaving the house behind before he could say another word. *'I'm not sure where I'm going or what I'm doing... I just know I can't sit still and stay here!'*

The morning sun shines down on me as my head hangs low. I feel empty, restless, annoyed and the only thing... The only person on my mind is her. That lady that's been making me feel the way I do. I see memories of her so I know she has something to do with my past, but the feelings she stirred inside me I can't explain. "Heh, well well look what I found stranded on the streets. It's the all high and mighty Kris Dolson!" I keep walking, *'The fuck is with that guy!'* Suddenly my arm was grabbed and I was pulled back. I feel my eye twitch as I stand tall facing the man who has a death wish. "Yo! What the hell is your problem! First you show up at my engagement party with some chick and now you're walking the streets and ignoring me!" *'Ahh that's that guy from last night... I think his name was Derick!'* "You were talking to me?" "I don't see anyone else here!" Derick let go of my arm. "But Kris I really need to thank you, if it wasn't for you coming with that girl Robin wouldn't have accepted my proposal!" He starts to walk off to go hop back into his car, but before he gets the chance to put a foot in I quickly slam the car door shut. “Why do you act like you know me and keep calling me Kris?”

He stares at me dumbfounded, "Heh, you're joking right? Our family has been competitors for years now, how could I not know you? You were also my rival in love!" *'This guy is hurting my head more than it did before!'* My hand slides off his door and presses against my temple hoping to relieve some of the pain in my head as my lost memories appear one by one flooding my mind... it won't stop! I feel my body sway as my legs go weak, I'm suddenly consumed into the forgotten past.

CHAPTER THIRTEEN

Back at Preuett's mansion, chaos has arisen as both the Preuett and Lee families have gathered into the living room to talk about their children, who have now gone MIA for almost a whole month and a half. Rex steps into the room of vocal parents. "Mrs. Lee, since we were informed on the whereabouts of Miss Robin and the mess Derick had gotten her into with the news of a wedding spreading like wildfire, as the head butler of the family, I will go to France and find a way to bring them both home. If all fails, I can at least keep you updated on how things are going. With that said, I would like to bring Miss Melissa as well since she is Miss Robin's maid?" Mrs. Lee tilts her head, thanking over his words as she looks up at her husband. "Connor dear, that doesn't sound like a bad idea. Plus, I'm worried sick for my dear daughter in law." Connor chuckles as he wraps his arms around Jade. "You are more worried about our son's fiancée than your own son?" "Well of course I'm worried about him too!" She lays her head on his chest sighing. "Well it's settled then!" Rose chimes in, grabbing her husband, Daniel's, arm. "But I would love it if Rex took my butler Charlie as well, I would love to get updates too you know!" Charlie bows to the couples giving a side glance at Rex, a sly grin growing on his face. "It would be my pleasure to assist them!"

CHAPTER FOURTEEN

Robin

'Shit! Shit! Shit! What the hell am I going to do!' I sat on the floor in front of the toilet, my knees pulled up to my chest as the test hangs from my hand, a plus sign showing bright as day and it didn't take long to show. I ended up staying in the bathroom through the night full of worry. I slowly stand on my feet swaying and stumble to the sink. My eyes look sunken in, my face pale as a ghost. I place the test to the side as I wash my face in the sink. *'I can't be like this! I'm going to tell Derick and he can either throw me out or give me a place to stay and if he still wants me... I'll go through with it!'* I stand tall, building my courage, my hand gripping the test as I turn, unlock the door and swing it open. *'No matter what, I'll do anything for this child!'*

I'm standing in the living room dumbfounded... he's nowhere to be found! *'Great, just when I've come up with a plan he's nowhere in the house... and I've searched everywhere!'* In the corner of my eyes I spot Edmé. Relieved to see someone familiar, I called out to him. He walks over to me and gives me a little bow. "How may I help you Miss?" "Have you seen Derick anywhere, I need to talk to him! It's an emergency!" I looked around trying to hide the test so I'm not ratted out. "I'm sorry ma'am but the master has left for a bit, though he should be back soon." *'The fuck! I was in the bathroom having a meltdown and he left me!'* I was about to throw my test to the ground and head out the door when it unexpectedly opened. *'Good! Now you'll get my wrath in person!'* I bolted up to him once he entered but froze in place seeing the man he and his driver were holding up in their arms.

"What the hell!" Fear and anger rose through me as I stood outside the door of the guest room to the one person I didn't want to see at all... Kris Preuett! The man that broke my heart! I just came to a conclusion about my life and here he is showing up again giving me a feeling I don't want. "Relax, I have a doctor coming to check on him and then we are kicking him out!" Derick moves closer to me but I shove him off. "No, my anger isn't just due to the fact you brought him here but you left!" I feel my eyes water so I bite my bottom lip. *'No! No more tears!'* I noticed his eyes soften as he grabbed a bag off the console table and pulled out a tub of brownie chunk ice cream. I stare at it feeling foolish! I lower my head and lean into his chest, "We need to talk!"

With the doctor in the room with Kris, we took our leave and sat down in the living room. I'm slowly nibbling on the ice cream trying to distract myself from the fact my test is sitting on the coffee table and Derick, who's sitting on the couch across from me, hasn't said a word... he just keeps staring between me and the test with his arms crossed. "You know this tension isn't helping my nerves!" I hear him sigh leaning forward on the couch, his arms leaning against his legs as his hands are balled up into a fist... a tight fist! His eyes narrow as he looks me dead in the eyes. "Let me explain something to you! I love you so much so you should know I'd do anything for you and this child would be like my own if you are willing to go through with this wedding with me!" The ice cream and spoon slipped out of my hands, startled by his words. Quickly I go to pick it up but he grabs me, not caring about the mess I just caused. "Robin, if you truly love him I'll let you go! Even so-" I move my hands over his lips looking back down at the mess on the floor. "He doesn't want me and I've hurt you from the time we were together. I'm willing to try this if you really will accept me and this child!" Before I knew it I was picked up off the floor, his face buried in my neck. "I can't tell you how happy this makes me feel!"

The doctor walks in and clears his throat. "I'm sorry to bother you Mr. Abernathy, but may I have a word with you?" Derick sets me back down on the couch and lightly kisses my head before walking into the hall with the doctor. I moved over to pick up the melted ice cream, but Colette had already stepped over and was cleaning up the mess. "Can I help in any way?" She smiles up at me, shaking her head. "No ma'am, it's almost done!" I slowly nod, apologizing for my clumsiness, and look back at the hall. I notice Derick looking at me... a face that gives me an unsettling feeling.

He comes back over and grabs my hands with a smile on his face. "Would you like to go out and eat with me my dear?" He says as his thumb strokes against my cheek. Grabbing his hand I pulled it close to my stomach, nodding my head. "I would love to, I hope you don't mind but I'm kinda craving pizza!" He tilts his head, giving a light chuckle. "Well I guess a fancy dinner isn't what you had planned!" He picks me up and calls out to his driver to start the car as we head out.

We're sitting down in a booth at a pizza restaurant and I can't help but sway as I wait for my pepperoni garlic pizza. The smells around the place and the thought of it makes me drool. "Heh, someone's excited!" Derick reaches over and wipes away my saliva with a napkin, causing me to look down fluster. *'What's wrong with me!'* It doesn't take long for the food to arrive and my eyes shine with excitement looking down at the source of my cravings. The moment the smell hit my nose I grabbed a slice without thinking and sank my teeth into it, the taste melting on my tongue.

I'm swaying in my sweat eating each slice, every bit getting better and better. I was so caught up in the food I failed to notice Derick looking at me. "Is there something on my face?" I say, grabbing a napkin and whipping my lips. His eyes soften as he sets down his phone. "You're perfect! Even with food on your face!" He gives a smile that slowly turns into a frown. Tilting my head I ask, "What's wrong?" He placed his hands on the table, balling them up into a fist. "Robin, I heard from the doctors how Kris is doing..." He trails off, his gaze drifting away from me. Placing my pizza down I can't help but shake my legs nervously. "What if I were to tell you that Kris had amnesia?" My jaw dropped, my head started to spin. *'Kris has lost his memory? When was this?'* My mind jumps back to the bridal shower when his eyes were filled with confusion. *'Oh my god!'*

CHAPTER FIFTEEN

Kris

Steadily sitting up in bed I tried to focus on my vision that was going in and out. I felt like I was asleep for weeks! "Ugg, I need the bathroom!" Gripping the sheets I rise off the bed and begin to walk to the closet door near me using the wall to support my every step, my head spinning. Twisting the knob, I shove open the door and then stumble over my feet. I grabbed onto the door to attempt to steady myself, only to have it break off its hinges under my weight. Breathing in a deep breath I stand tall and toss the door to the side. I look up, facing into a mirror, to find how pale I have now become. I lean over the sink, splashing my face with the water trying to get my mind on track. *'I was walking and then what? Ahh Derick showed up... but then everything went black!'* I look back out into the room. *'Where the hell is this place!'* I spotted a window then treaded over to it, yanking down the curtains, on the other side was a huge backyard and the sea further out in view. I can feel my eyes twitch as I become annoyed with this unknown place.

I hear the door knobs turn and creak open, through the glass I could see an older man wearing a white coat and a stethoscope around his neck walk in. "Ahh good, you've awoken! Please sit so I can check your vitals!" He gestures to the bed. Thinning my lips I go along with it, placing myself back on the bed. After a bit he moves away nodding his head. "Well sir, can you tell me your name?" He grabs his clipboard and scans through the papers. I lean over on my legs using my arms as support, "Kris Preuett!" Looking at him, he just keeps nodding his head. "It seems like everything is ok, I did some scans the past few days to make sure you had no other injuries, and it seems you have regained your memory back so I'd say you are good to go! Let me just call Mr. Abernathy and keep him updated on your progress." He turns from me but I quickly stand and grab onto his shoulder. "Hold up! You need to answer a few questions on what the fuck you mean past few days and why the hell you need to talk to Derick!"

He stares at me, beads of sweat starting to drip down his face. "W...Well sir Kris, Derick had brought you to his home when you fainted and had called for me and my colleagues to come and check on you... Take care of you! You've been sleeping for five days. If... If you don't mind sir I do need to be going, I do have other appointments!" He backs away, gripping on to his clipboard. My eyes strayed from his face to the paperwork. "Before you go give me those health documents! Oh, and also where is my fiancé?" His eyebrows furrowed as he hesitantly handed me my medical records. "Robin! I'm looking for my fiancé Robin!"

Walking down the hall behind the doctor, I can hear my steps echo as they slam onto the floor, my eyes darken. Where near the living room and the doc parts from me heading out the front door as I stand there refusing to take another step. A different man approaches me, who I assume is the butler of this home. "Ahh sir Kris, it's a pleasure to see you up and going!" He says as he gives a slight bow. "How may I help you sir?" Scanning the area, I ask, "Where's Derick and Robin?" "Master Derick and Miss Robin are out at the moment!" My teeth grind together as I feel my eyes begin to twitch. Without another word I go over and sit on the couch crossing my arms. "Well I'll wait here for them then, can you bring me some water!" He bows again, "Certainly sir!" Then walks off.

Hours pass and the front door swings open to laughter echoing throughout the mansion. I sit there as two figures walk into the living room. They stopped in their tracks, spotting me. Fear grows in the woman's eyes as she turns to scurry off. Flying off the couch I grab her, pulling her back into my chest, my arms wrapping around her waist, and my face nuzzling into her neck. "I've missed you!" She begins to shiver in my arms making me squeeze onto her a bit tighter. *'This... This is what I was missing. She feels perfect to me!'* She doesn't struggle, only slips out light sobs under her breath. "Why? Why do you like messing with my head so much? Why when I have a problem solved you always seem to screw it up? Why is it that as much as I want to hate you and am finally ok being away from you, you always make me fall for you deeper than before?" Smiling into her neck I whispered, "You're the only woman I love, even without my memories I felt empty. Nothing felt right! I'm so sorry if I hurt you!" My hand slides under her chin, pushing her head back to look up at me. My eyes closed as I softly kissed her lips!

I feel her kiss me back, her body leaning up against me as her shivering calms down. We stay like this for a while, savoring every moment until Derick butts in by clearing his throat. "Um... well then I guess I'm rejected once again!" He chuckled, but you could hear the disappointment in his tone. "Oh my god I'm so sorry!" Robbin looks down flustered and attempts to pull away from me. I noticed her ears were a bright red color so I leaned in and nipped her ear. "Hey! Kris! What are you doing?" She pouts as she covers her ears. My eyes soften as I watch her, forgetting about Derick's presence. *'She's so damn cute!'* "Master Derick, you have some guests at the door!" Edmé announces before heading back to the entrance.

CHAPTER SIXTEEN

The plane ride took a while, but it was full of tension. Melissa stayed to herself in a window seat, scribbling things down in her notebook and looking out the window, mumbling to herself as Rex and his brother Charlie sipped on their martinis. Charlie looks at Melissa with a small smile on his face. "She's so cute! Must be lucky to get to see her everyday!" Twirling his drink, Rex scoffs. "I knew you weren't coming to help find master Kris and Miss Robin." "Can you blame me for taking advantage of the situation brother? I have the right to captivate the women I love!" Rex's eyes narrowed at Charlie's words, but before he could speak Melissa came rushing over, grabbing onto Rex's arm with a smile on her face. "I made some calls and I found the location of Abernathy's private home!"

She hurries off to the pilot and gives him directions to the mansion, before rushing back to her seat, picking up her book and putting in her headphones, ignoring the men. After some time had passed, they had landed on Derick's home garden. Once landed, they descended off the plane as a man walked out of the mansion. "Welcome to Abernathy's home! I'm Edmé, the head butler of this home. Sir Kris and Miss Robin are right this way!" He leads us to the entrance and tells us to wait just a moment. "Heh at least this was quick, just sad we didn't get to spend more time together!" Charlie leans his head on Melissa's shoulder. She moves over, simply brushing him off. "Remember Chaz, we are here for business!" She scowled at him before she looked back at the door.

CHAPTER SEVENTEEN

Robin

I was trying to keep my mind straight but my nerves kept getting in the way, causing me to feel nauseous. Struggling to be released from his arms I shouted, "Please let go!" Startled, he frees me from his grasp, giving me the chance to run into the bathroom, vomiting into the toilet. I hadn't noticed Derick and Kris had followed behind me till I felt a hand on my back and someone holding up my hair, Kris asking in worry, "Oh my god Robin, are you ok?" Derick moves away from my side then leans against the wall crossing his arms smiling. "Aren't you in for a surprise!"

Once back in the living room, I'm sipping on some water as Kris sticks by my side with his hand glued to my thigh. "So, tell me, what's the surprise?" I look at Derick chewing on my bottom lip. "Hey Derick, can you get that thing from my room? It's on the dresser!" He scurried off, giving me a chance to look at the guests that showed up before. Those I haven't seen in so long. I reach out, grabbing Melissa's hands. "How have y'all been? How are my parents?" She smiles and begins to speak, telling me all was well, and how I have nothing to worry about. Feeling at peace, I sit back and relax a bit, finally being able to breathe. Even so, it wasn't long until Derick was back in the room. He sat next to me secretly sliding the test into my hands. I moved my body to fully face Kris dead in his face, taking in a deep breath as my heart rate began to spike. I slowly raised my hands revealing the test to him and announced, "I'm pregnant with your child!"

His eyes are locked on the pregnancy test, causing my anxiety to increase with every passing moment. "Um... well I still need to go get a checkup and we don't know the gender yet. There's also the fact that we still-" He grabs me, pulling me into his chest, his arms tightly wrapping around me, I hear him lightly sob. *'Is... Is he crying?'* 'Robin, I can't explain how ecstatic I am to hear this news! Our first child!" His hands moved to cup my face, having me look up at him, tears filled in his eyes. "This child and you will forever be my everything!" He whispers as he lightly kisses my lips.

After a bit more time of catching up and Kris composing his emotions and with me dying to get back home, we had finally gotten to where we needed to say our farewells to the Abernathy family, though it felt wrong to leave little June as she held onto me with tears streaming down her little cheeks. Seeing her like that had brought me to tears myself and hugged her for a while. Leaning back in my seat on the plane I thought back on these weeks since I had arrived. My hands slide over my stomach gently rubbing it. *'Not long ago I thought he would want nothing to do with us anymore!'* I look over at Kris, his eyes closed, his chest slowly rising and falling with each breath he takes. I can't take my eyes off him. "I've missed you too!"

My hand drops from my side causing me to wake up in a startle. "Hold on love, don't move around too much!" Looking around, I find I'm being held close to Kris's chest. He walks us inside his home and into the living room, where he lightly sets me down. "How are you feeling?" He brings me a cover and places a pillow behind me. "I'm feeling fine!" I say, rubbing my eyes, yawning. "Ok, our parents are in the other room, if you're feeling up for it I'll let them in and I'll go get you some water!" I nodded my head groggily. He smiles and kisses my head then tucks the cover around me before leaving the room.

All was peaceful, causing me to nod off again, but it was disrupted once our parents were in the room. There was crying and wailing echoing in the room causing me to panic a tad bit. Arms had surrounded me in the midst of my confusion but after a few moments I was able to comprehend their presence, hugging everyone tightly with tears in my own eyes. When everything was settled, we talked about everything that's been going on since I've been gone... though there was one thing I did leave out. Kris came back after what felt like forever. He sits down by my side pulling me in and passing me the glass of water. I take a sip as he speaks, "So what did I miss? Did you tell them the-" I coughed on the water, cutting him off, knowing what he was going to say. They all surrounded me once more, worried. I waved my free hand, placing the cup down and looking down, grabbing onto Kris's arm. "Um... Well, I was waiting for you to come back!" I look up at everyone taking a deep breath. "You all are going to be grandparents!"

The moment those words slipped past my lips, they were stunned, looking at each other then at us before staring down at my stomach before simultaneously talking to me and Kris, about what? I'm not even sure. Being surrounded by them all I could feel my anxiety creeping up bringing along another little queasy feeling. I tapped on Kris a few times before standing up off the couch and sprinting for the restroom. *'I guess that's one way to escape from socializing!'*

After a few moments my mother walks into the bathroom as I sit on the floor taking deep breaths, in with my nose and out with my mouth. "Some salted crackers and ginger ale should help with the feeling dear!" She sits down next to me, passing the snacks and a drink over to me. She leans on the wall sitting on the ground with me, moving over after taking a sip, I scooch over to be next to her and lean on her. "I've missed you so much!" I said with a small smile. Her hand wraps around my cheek as she leans her head onto mine. "I've missed you dear!" We sat there by each other, in the peaceful silence and with the warmth of my mother I felt at peace and comfort. My eyes became heavy and before I knew it, I was lightly snoring on my mother's shoulder.

CHAPTER EIGHTEEN

Kris

It was silent in the bathroom and it was causing my nervousness to fill me from within. I rushed in to see both Robin and her mother on the floor. Mrs. Lee places a finger to her lips shushing me as her daughter sleeps soundly on her side. I step over and crouch down to them. "How is she?" I whisper. Mrs. Lee slowly stands as I pull Robbin into my chest, lightly picking her up cradling her. "She's perfectly fine, just a little nauseous!" She smiles looking down at her daughter, "Please take good care of her!" She gently kisses Robin before leaving us.

I walk us to our room and lay her on the bed, tucking her in. After watching her for a few minutes to make sure she would be ok, I turned to the bathroom, but my hand was grabbed. I look down at her hand gripping tightly around mine. "Please don't leave me!" She looks up at me slowly moving to her knees and leaning towards the edge of the bed. I move closer, not wanting her to fall. "I'm not leaving hun, I was just going to take a shower!" I moved in closer, giving her a kiss on the lips, then went to move again but was pulled on top of the bed, Robin straddling my lap. She stares down at me, her waist gradually grinding against me, causing my cock to harden beneath her. Grabbing her waist, I'm trying to hold her back. "Hun, we just got back, and you must be exhausted." *'Plus, with everything that has happened I am just happy to have her back with me, even though I would love to embrace her!'* I tried to sit up and move her off of me, but was shoved back down, her lips pressed up against mine. Welcoming this kiss, my tongue slips through her lips, pushing against hers.

My pants suddenly became unbuttoned and my cock was pulled out. I couldn't help but groan as she rubbed me. Pulling away from the kiss I look into her eyes. "Are you sure about this hun?" She nibbles my bottom lip. "Kris, I don't think you understand how much I've missed you and how bad I really want you right now!" She sits up, strips off her shirt and bra, throwing them to the side. She grabs my hands as she's leaning back down to me, her lips inches away from mine as she slides my hands over her soft breasts, feeling her warmth beneath my fingertips. "I crave you, Kris!" She whispers before kissing me deeply. Squeezing her breasts, I flip us over to where I tower over her and rip off the rest of her clothing, unable to hold back my patients. I trace a hand down her stomach and in between her legs, my fingers tracing small patterns on her inner thigh causing her breathing to hitch.

"I hope you know you started something that you will not be able to stop!" I say, licking my lips as my fingers trail further up her thigh to her pussy, my thumb brushing against her clit. I can hear her let out a small whimper making me ache with desire. “Mmm I love hearing those little sounds of yours.” Using my other hand I grip her thigh, widening her legs for me to slide between them as my thumb begins to circling with increasing pressure on her sensitive spot. “It drives me crazy.”

I'm between her legs licking between her lips, her juices overflowing the more aggressive I get with my tongue going deeper and deeper inside her pussy. Her fingers slide through my hair, tugging as she moans, "Kris Please fuck me! I want to feel your cock deep inside me!" Smirking, I sit up, lifting one of her legs over my shoulder as I pull her down, closer to where my hard, throbbing length is pressed firmly against her dripping wet folds, the tip teasing her entrance. "Is my honey wanting this?" "Fuck it, if you won't...." She lifts herself up, pushing me back down on my back, lust clouding her eyes as her fingers wrap around my cock steadily sliding the tip inside her. "Then I will!" She pushes down on my cock, arching her back as she bites on her bottom lip. Groaning, I grip her waist firmly, lifting her up then back down on my cock. "Damn baby you feel so good!" She starts to bounce faster on me, leaning back on her arms while using my legs to support her. I feel her core tighten on my cock making me moan as I watch her breasts sway hypnotically. It was so enticing I couldn't help but lean in to wrap my lips and tongue over her nipple sucking while she had her way with me. *'Fuck I love this woman so damn much!'*

'I tried hard not to overdo it but this woman was so aggressive in bed!' Leaning over her sleeping body I kissed her lips before sliding out of bed, sliding on my jeans and heading out the door. I'm storming down the hall and opening the door to my office. "Rex bring me all the information for the past few weeks of my company, also send Melissa to check up on Robin and take her scrambled eggs with a side of toast and a fruit bowl... ah and a glass of water!" Once in the room I sit behind my desk as Rex hurries in, placing all the paperwork down. "And the food?" I ask, leaning back in my chair. "Melissa sent it right up sir!" "Good! That'll be all!" I waved him off, picking up a stack of documents.

Sighing, I place my head into my hands, feeling my head begin to throb. *'I can't even focus on work at the moment!'* I look over at the rest of the papers that've been left untouched. "All I want is her..." I say under my breath. Suddenly a knocking comes from the door and it creaks open, a head popping through it. "Um.... I'm sorry if I'm bothering you... but it was lonely in the room without you!" She takes a few steps into the room, her head hanging low with her arms behind her back. I watched as she stumbled on her words and nibbled on her bottom lip, her cheeks growing red. I move off the chair and am swiftly in front of her. My arm wraps around her waist as a hand lifts her chin up, having her look deeply into my eyes. I feel her hands grasp my shirt as her breathing becomes unsteady and before I can do anything else she lifts herself on her toes and kisses me. "Kris, let's get married!"

Staring at her confused, a slight smile grows on my face. I pick her up and her legs instantly wrap around my waist as I do. "What day would you like it hun?" She pursed her lips as she moved her arms around my neck, thinking. I walk her over to my desk shoving the papers to the side allowing her to be able to sit down. She leans back on her arms, "I want it as soon as possible and if we could I'd rather have a small wedding!" She smiles up at me, pulling me in closer with her legs. "Can't have any more interruptions in our relationship can we?" Her eyes narrow as her smile turns into a smirk. "Mmm hun..." I pushed her back into the desk kissing her, my hands sliding under my shirt she seemed to have stolen.

"Sweetie, it's mommy! We need to talk-" My mother stops in her tracks and stares at us, her face becoming flushed before she runs back out of the room. *'Well that killed the mood!'* Looking back down at Robin, she covers her face. "Um.... I'm going to get dressed and meet y'all downstairs!" She sits up, sliding to the other side of the desk, and scurries out of the room as fast as she can. I couldn't help but chuckle seeing how red her ears were as she left.

CHAPTER NINETEEN

Robin

'What's going on with me, I've never been this upfront before!' Holding my flushed face, I hurry into the bathroom stripping off what little clothes I have on and turning on the shower, drenching myself in the cold water trying to calm my racing heart. *'His mom even saw us like that! Oh my god!'* "I'm sorry to interrupt Miss, but I'm here to inform you that dinner is ready, along with both yours and master Kris's parents are here for a family meal!" "Ah ok... Give me a few moments and I'll be right down!" I get no response but do hear the sound of the door closing, leaving me in my mind swarming with worry and distress, causing my breathing to become unsteady. *'I don't think I can face his mother!'*

After the hot steaming shower I step into the room, the

towel tightly wrapped around my body covering my curves. I take in a deep breath, feeling more relaxed. Humming a light tune I head over to the closet wondering what I should wear for dinner. "Honey, I have a beautiful dress I'd love for you to wear tonight!" Arms gently slide around my waist, a warm sensation touches my back as I feel his breath on my neck. His touch sends shivers up my spine. "Hehe! Hello my love, what dress would that be?" I turn around in his arms, my fingers trace across his skin. "I have it over on the bed, but I think we should finish what we started before!" He kisses up my neck before nibbling on my ear causing me to slip a soft moan. "But darling, aren't our parents waiting for us?" We start to sway as we move over to where my back is against the wall. "They can wait a bit longer!" His lips trace from my ear to my lips as he moves his hand from my waist down to my thigh, pulling my leg up to his side. I grip his shirt, letting my towel fall to the floor as we kiss, our tongues intertwining. My hands trace over his broad chest down to the rim of his paints, tugging lightly on it. "Then we better make this quick!" I say it under my breath, unzipping his pants then pulling out his cock, my fingers gently wrapping around it, feeling the warmth and as it twitches in her grasp. Slowly I began to stroke it, my thumb rubbing against the tip. His breathing becomes ragged as he begins to thrust it into my hand. "Oh baby that feels good," As he inches his clock closer to my pussy I nibble on my bottom lip as it rubs against my pink folds. "but I want to be deep inside you, I want to hear that arousing moan of yours!" He grabs on to my other leg as I steady his cock into my opening. He pushes it further into me as his lips devour mine, his grip on my thighs tightening. "Then fuck me baby!" I murmur into the kiss, my legs wrapping around his waist causing him to shove his cock fully inside me. I could feel it slowly sliding in and out of me, each thrust picking up speed faster and faster, my moans growing louder with each thrust. I slide my hands up under his shirt, my nails scraping his back. "Ah Robin, I love you!" He grunts in my ear as he pushes his hard length deeper inside me. "Kris, I love you so much!"

"Ahh! They finally showed up for dinner!" Mr. Preuett says with open arms as he rises from his seat at the table. "Heh! I'm sorry father, we had some private matters we needed to attend to!" Following behind Kris I can't help but blush from his comment. He pulls out a chair for me to sit in before sitting right next to me. As they talked amongst themselves a maid had come over pouring water into a glass for me and Kris. I grasp it and bring it to my lips, taking sips from it. In the midst of commotion, Kris interrupts the happy group by clicking on a wine glass as he rises from his seat, "Parents... We are getting married!" I started to choke on the water a bit startled from his actions. *'I know I'm the one who said I wanted to get married, but I didn't know we were telling them now!'* "Um... I am sorry to cut in, but I do have a request for this wedding!" Kris is patting my back as I look around the room with a stern look. "I want this wedding to be small and with that I want it to be as soon as possible!" I look up at him. "I know you wanted a big wedding, and my wants may be selfish, but I'm ready to settle down with you and our child!" I say, caressing my stomach. *'Our past wedding when I was still on the fence on how I felt, I was forced into it only to realize at death's door I truly wanted to be by this man. No more mistakes, no more wasting time! No more interruptions!'* "Kris, I want you and only you! I've loved you since we were kids, but instead of expressing that I pulled away from you time and time again!" I stand, sliding a hand over his cheek, my face inches from his. "I'm so sorry for how long it took for me to figure that out and for everything I had put you through!" He shakes his head. "Hun, it was not on you, I shouldn't have been so controlling and forced you... I... I just couldn't stand the thought of losing you and I would do anything to keep you in my life!" We kissed, he pulled me closer to him. As we part, I stare down awkwardly as the parents have now moved in closer to us. "Great, then me and Mrs. Preuett will start planning!" The two women say, grabbing my arms and pulling me away from Kris. "Know, what are your thoughts and what is the theme for the wedding?" My mother asks. "Ohhhh we should go dress shopping immediately!" Mrs. Preuett chimes in.

After several weeks with maids and butlers running all over the mansion, crazy shopping trips with ecstatic mothers, doctor appointments... along with possibly very arousing nights, our wedding day has finally approached, along with my belly bulging further. I stare out my room window looking out into the backyard seeing the full wedding layout and people scattering like ants. I place my hand over my chest as my nervousness finally begins to kick in. *'We're finally here!'* A knock comes from the door and Melissa walks in holding a box. "What is that?" She walks up to me, passing it into my arms. "It's a gift from master Kris!" I walk over to the bed, lightly placing it down and unraveling the bow before pulling off the lid revealing a white gown, with a note saying, "Let's give it a second chance and do this right!" Pulling the dress out of the box, I couldn't help the tears that fell down my cheeks. *'This... it's the same dress!'* My fingers traced over the silky fabric. "Would you like some help putting it on Miss?" Melissa placed her hand on my back. Nodding my head, she grabs the dress from my hands. I move in front of the mirror to slip off my shirt and skirt. She helps me slide the dress over my head and lets it fall over me like it did before. It looked just the same, but with a few adjustments. "Master Kris had it remade along with some room for the belly bump!" She says as I stare into the mirror, lost for words. Overwhelmed with emotion, I quickly turned to Melissa, wrapping my arms around her neck, crying.

"Oh dear! What has saddened our bride to be?" Mrs. Preuett and my mother enter the room and upon noticing the state I am in, they become distressed, pulling me off my maid and checking me from head to toe. "Did you get hurt? Is there a problem with the baby? Is the dress messed up?" Shaking my head frantically I try to speak through my sobs. "Nothing.... Nothing is wrong! I'm... I'm just so happy... after what happened in this... this dress before, I now have another chance to wear something... something this beautiful Kris picked out for me!" They looked at one another with relief. My mother sighs with a smile and caresses my cheeks, wiping away my tears. "Sweetie there is no need for tears, it's a happy day and you still need your hair and makeup done!" Mrs. Preuett then chimes in, "and since the last wedding attempt my son has been taking extra precautions that today will be perfect, and he remembers how distraught you were when... when you were injured in the dress!" They moved me to the vanity, sitting me down in the chair. "Know your mother will do your makeup, while I fix your lovely blonde hair dear!" I can't help but sniffle and nod, my smile growing. "Thank you both so much!"

Fully dressed, hair and makeup done, I'm standing by the back door. My heart is racing with a mix of anxiety and happiness. I'm trying to focus on my breathing when a hand places itself on my shoulder causing me to jump from shock. "Oh! I'm sorry if I scared you!" My father stares down at me with a tender smile. "Are you going to be ok, we can head to another room and sit for a bit if you like?" I smile from my father's presents and with his concern. *'My parents were always good to me and spoiled me with so much love and affection. I know in the past they promised me to Kris, but if they had another way, they would have taken it and it's not like they left me or disowned me... in fact they were always there, but I was so concerned with my own selfishness that I disregarded them without realizing!'* Grabbing my dad, I pulled him in, hugging him tightly. "Dad I'm so sorry for my childish ways and for always pushing you and mom away!" He raised my chin to look up at him, and for once in my life I've found tears in my father's eyes. "My sweet girl, you have nothing to feel sorry about! You are a wonderful, strong, independent young lady! I know me and your mother have put you in a tough situation and we deeply apologize for that, but we will never leave your side! And if he mistreats you in any way, you better come home to us, and we will give him a thing or two... well with a little help from his parents of course." I heard him chuckle and let me say this was definitely the comfort I needed. "Ok dad," I say, taking a deep breath and breaking the hug. "I think I'm ready!" I held out my arm with a big smile on my face. He kisses my cheek and pulls down my veil before sliding his arm around mine. We walk closer to the door and my father opens it for us, welcoming the bright sundown on us.

Everything happened in a blur, I walked down the aisle giving no glance to those in the crowd, my eyes focused on Kris. When we get to the stand, my father kisses my cheek one last time before leaving my side and me face to face with my soon to be husband. I paid no mind to the words the officiant had said... well only to the part when I needed to say I do and the exchanging of rings. During the whole time I was trying so hard not to cry and freak out in a panic, my mind swarming with so many negative thoughts. "Honey!" I failed to notice Kris had closed in the gap, our hands entwined with one another. He whispers again, "Honey, are you ok?" Lightly I nodded my head. "I'm... I'm ok!" He smiles brightly at my words then removes his hand from mine to remove the veil between us. "Good!" Is all I hear from him before his lips are against mine. "Ladies and gentlemen, it is my pleasure to present to you Mr. and Mrs. Preuett!"

www.ingramcontent.com/pod-product-compliance
Lightning Source LLC
LaVergne TN
LVHW090526110826
845146LV00003B/993

* 9 7 9 8 2 3 4 0 3 2 8 8 1 *